Talker's Town

and

The Girl Who Swam Forever

ALSO BY MARIE CLEMENTS

*Burning Vision**

*Copper Thunderbird**

The Edward Curtis Project: A Modern Picture Story
   (with Rita Leistner)*

*Tombs of the Vanishing Indian**

*The Unnatural and Accidental Women**

*PUBLISHED BY TALONBOOKS

Talker's Town

and

The Girl Who Swam Forever

Two Plays

NELSON GRAY

and

MARIE CLEMENTS

Talonbooks

Talonbooks
278 East First Avenue, Vancouver, British Columbia, Canada V5T 1A6
talonbooks.com

First printing: 2018

Typeset in Arno
Printed and bound in Canada on 100% post-consumer recycled paper

Cover illustrations by Alan Hindle. Endpaper illustrations by Chloë Filson
Interior design by Typesmith.

Rights to produce *Talker's Town*, in whole or in part, in any medium by any group, amateur or professional, are retained by the author. Interested persons are requested to contact Talonbooks at 278 East First Avenue, Vancouver, British Columbia, Canada V5T 1A6; telephone (toll-free) 888-445-4176; email: info@talonbooks.com; talonbooks.com.

Rights to produce *The Girl Who Swam Forever*, in whole or in part, in any medium by any group, amateur or professional, are retained by the author. Interested persons are kindly requested to contact Marie Clements, P.O. Box 2662, Vancouver Main, Vancouver, British Columbia, V6B 3W8; telephone 778-881-3801.

The Girl Who Swam Forever was previously published in *Footpaths and Bridges: Voices from the Native American Women Playwrights Archive* by the University of Michigan Press in 2008.

Talonbooks acknowledges the financial support of the Canada Council for the Arts, the Government of Canada through the Canada Book Fund, and the Province of British Columbia through the British Columbia Arts Council and the Book Publishing Tax Credit.

LIBRARY AND ARCHIVES CANADA CATALOGUING IN PUBLICATION

Talker's town and The girl who swam forever : two plays / Marie Clements and Nelson Gray.

Talker's town written by Nelson Gray; The girl who swam forever written by Marie Clements.
ISBN 978-1-77201-201-9 (SOFTCOVER)

1. One-act plays, Canadian (English). 2. Canadian drama (English)--21st century. I. Gray, Nelson, 1952- . Talker's town. II. Clements, Marie, 1962- . Girl who swam forever.

PS8309.O5T35 2018   C812'.0410806   C2018-901466-0

CONTENTS

PREFACE

When I was fifteen, a bunch of friends and I were driving around on a Saturday night in a small mill town where nothing ever happened. It was pitch dark – no street lamps – and the rain, which was coming down in sheets, was pooling up on the pavement. My sixteen-year-old friend – a decent, good-natured kid – was behind the wheel of his family's '55 Chevy when we came up behind a car that was going dead slow.

"That's John's car," said one of my friends, "I bet he thinks we're the cops and that he's being tailed." "Yeah – he's probably had a few, and he's afraid he's going to get pulled over."

"We should pass him," someone else chimed in.

I can't or maybe don't want to remember whether I was one of the chorus of voices that cheered on this idea. Within moments, though, the car was thrust into overdrive, my friend flooring it the way inexperienced drivers do when they're still nervous about passing.

Seconds later we saw them – three black coats stretched out across the road in front of us. My friend hit the brakes and the car slid out of control across the slick wet pavement. Three terrifying thuds. Two of the teenaged girls were left with broken bones and bruises. The third girl lay with her head in the gravel at the side of the road, killed on contact.

Trauma does strange things to memory.

The two surviving girls were members of the Katzie band, the First Nations People who lived on the reserve next to my home town. The girl who had been killed was not. She had skin that was darker than that of most of the kids in my high school, but she was not Indigenous.

Definitely not. And yet, for years afterwards, whenever memories of that horrific night revisited me, she was always, in my mind, a Katzie girl.

Perhaps this mistake was due to my memories of the inquest, where the parents of the injured Katzie girls sat alongside the grief-stricken family of the deceased girl, calling for justice from the coroner, a man who, as it seemed to me, was adopting a rather too sympathetic attitude in regards to us white kids. Perhaps it was because of how my feelings of complicity in the girl's death had melded with a vague apprehension of a resentment I had perceived among many Indigenous people, a resentment I felt might be directed towards me. Whatever the case, though, it was this mistaken memory, this misrecognition of a past event, that became the catalyst for *Talker's Town* – a play about a teenaged boy who feels responsible for a Katzie girl on the run from residential school, and, in turn, for Marie Clements's *The Girl Who Swam Forever*, a play that portrays the same sequence of events from the Indigenous girl's point of view.

I learned of my mistake in the early stages of writing *Talker's Town*, when I found an old high school album with a dedication to the girl who had been killed. I stared at her photograph in bewilderment. Not an Indigenous girl. Definitely not. By this time, though, I was already engaged in research about the Katzie People, research that was revealing an entirely different view of my hometown than the one I had carried with me for over twenty years.

On the week before the discovery of that high school album, I'd driven the road where the accident had occurred on my way to the one place in the vicinity of my home town I had always been uneasy about visiting: the Katzie reserve on the north bank of the Fraser River.

Jimmy Adams, a guy with a great sense of humour and the first person I met there, seemed anything but resentful. After hearing about my idea for the play, he regaled me for hours in his kitchen with stories of fishing on the Fraser and of his teenage years growing up on the reserve."If you want to know more about the Katzie though," Jimmy told me, "the person to talk to would be Agnes Pierre. Yeah, she'd be the one all right. You should definitely talk to her."

Jimmy's advice startled me and filled me with anticipation. Before coming to the reserve, I had been captivated by a collection of creation stories, as told by a Katzie Shaman named Old Pierre – by marriage, one of Agnes's ancestors, and the man responsible for one of the most significant records of Coast Salish traditions and cultures. In the 1930s the ethnographer Diamond Jenness, impressed by Old Pierre's extensive cultural knowledge, had transcribed his stories in a document titled *The Faith of a Coast Salish Indian*. Some twenty years later, another ethnographer, Wayne Suttles, published Jenness's transcriptions, alongside *Katzie Ethnographic Notes,* his own observations of Katzie life, based on conversations with Old Pierre's son, Simon.

The stories of Old Pierre and his son held particular meaning for me, deepening and enriching my understanding of the region where I had grown up. I learned, for instance, that the Fraser and Pitt Rivers, before the invading settler populations constructed dikes, had been a network of watery highways on which the Katzie People had travelled, and that the land my family and other settlers had farmed, with its lush green pastures and deep black loam, had formed over thousands of years from the silt of the river valley. I learned, too, that the mountains and caves and islands that I had explored as a boy had been the provenance of creation stories as rich and textured as the Genesis stories in the Bible or the mythic tales recounted by Hesiod and Homer. And I learned about the Katzie People's relationship with the sturgeon that had once been plentiful in the rivers and lakes of the area, fish that – as it happened – would come to play a prominent role in Marie's play.

When I showed up unannounced at Agnes Pierre's front door, she was understandably guarded, an attitude that didn't alter much when I explained the reason for my visit. As a residential school survivor, Agnes was not inclined to look kindly upon a white guy who had come looking for "material" for his play. Her suspicions continued when I told her of my familiarity with Old Pierre's stories, but after a few more visits to the reserve she seemed to think better of me, even granting me a recorded interview with her and several other Katzie Elders. When it came to Agnes's experiences at residential school, though, she remained quiet, and I knew enough not to pry. Once, when I had asked her to pronounce a word in her native Hul̓q̓umín̓um̓ language, she told me she still felt fearful doing so, lest an invisible hand poised over her shoulder might be ready to strike.

Thanks to Agnes, to Jimmy Adams, and to Diane Bailey – the then-presiding Chief of the Katzie band in Port Hammond – I was able to deepen my appreciation for the Katzie People and for their traditional cultural practices, and I continued to research their history and to learn more about the cruelties inflicted on Indigenous children and families as a result of residential schools. And yet, when I tried to bring the character of the Katzie girl into my play, I hit a stone wall: a classic case of writer's block.

Was this because of a lack of skill or imagination on my part or because I knew, in my gut, that I might be speaking with a voice that I had no right to appropriate? In retrospect, I think it may have been a bit of both. One thing was certain, however: my attempts at finding the voice for the Katzie girl were not working. Hers was a sensibility I could not, for the life of me, find a way to bring into my play in any substantive way.

"Have you heard of Marie Clements?" Kim Selody asked. I had sought out Kim, the Artistic Director of the New

Play Centre for some advice about how to get over my writer's block. "She's a Métis playwright who has been writing about Indigenous experience. She might be able to help you."

I met Marie at a coffee shop on Robson Street in Vancouver in 1994, and was immediately taken with her energy and charisma. At the time, my own writing and performing for the stage had been well received by critics and audiences, and my collaborations with choreographer and co-director Lee Eisler had met with considerable success on national and international tours. Marie, ten years younger than I, was just beginning to emerge as a playwright, yet her dynamism and drive were readily apparent, and, in the decades that followed, her accomplishments as an award-winning playwright, screenwriter, and director have been remarkable.

At our coffee meeting, I outlined the characters and plot line of my play, explained my difficulties with the character of the Katzie girl, and was both surprised and relieved when she offered to help. To fuel her enterprise, I loaned her my copy of *Katzie Ethnographic Notes*, along with Terry Glavin's *Ghost in the Water* – two books that included stories about the Katzie People's relationship with the sturgeon in Pitt Lake.

Some weeks later, when I met with Marie again, she let me know, in no uncertain terms, the extent of her annoyance. "I feel," she said, "as if I've been ghettoized in a white guy's play." I would have had to be pretty thick not to appreciate her position. "Of course," I said, "what you need to do is create your own play, but from the view of the Katzie girl."

Everything happened quickly after that. Marie agreed to the plan, I scraped up a bit of cash to commission the work, and several weeks later, Marie presented me with a first draft of *The Girl Who Swam Forever*.

If reading the stories of Old Pierre and talking with the Katzie had begun to open my eyes to Indigenous ways of seeing, Marie's play woke me up to the imaginative possibilities that could arise from such a world view. Her play had two parallel narratives. One of these stemmed from some of the situations and characters that I had been working with in *Talker's Town*, and – as promised – all of these had been re-drawn from the perspective of the Katzie girl. To ground this perspective, however, Marie had turned to one of Old Pierre's creation stories, creating a second narrative, a mythical, dreamlike one that counterpointed with the first. And, to give voice to this second narrative thread, she had channelled the voice of the girl's grandmother, but in the form of an enormous one-hundred-year-old sturgeon, who had awoken from sleep at the bottom of the river to provide strength and guidance for her granddaughter.

Reading *The Girl Who Swam Forever* was an uncanny experience for me. Here was a play portraying many of the same events and characters that I had been imagining, but viewed through a radically different cultural lens. It was as if I had passed through a portal to another version of my world, one that had always been there, but that I had never seen: sort of like when Alice steps through the looking-glass, except the looking-glass world that I had entered wasn't fantasy; it was a glimpse of the world I thought I had known, but that was now being informed by Indigenous history, Indigenous experience, and an Indigenous world view.

I was so captured by what Marie had written that I chose to direct *The Girl Who Swam Forever* as part of my degree requirements in Theatre at the University of British Columbia, and so entranced with how the two plays spoke to one another that, after graduating, I did everything I could to convince Marie to merge the two plays into an evening-length production. The experience of directing

Marie's play was a pleasure from start to finish. The attempt to combine the two plays proved difficult, however, and afterwards we parted ways, with each of us taking what we'd learned to revise our own plays for independent productions.

What I later came to realize, though, is that these two plays are most effective and most engaging when presented as a kind of diptych: two distinct, one-act plays, each occupying their own ground, and enacting, through the juxtaposition of their differences, a cross-cultural dialogue.

It seems obvious to me now that in writing *Talker's Town* and in reaching out to the Katzie People and to Marie Clements, I was attempting to account not only for the death of that young girl and for the injuries to those two Katzie girls, but also for the socially and historically constructed racism that continues to plague attitudes and institutions in this country.

In the early 1990s, when Marie and I were at work on *Talker's Town* and *The Girl Who Swam Forever*, there had been no parliamentary apologies for the abuses of residential schools, no United Nations Declaration on the Rights of Indigenous Peoples, no Truth and Reconciliation Commission, no National Inquiry into Missing and Murdered Indigenous Women and Girls. It might even be said that over the last couple of decades, history has to some extent been catching up with the subject matter of these plays. It is my hope, then, that our decision to publish *Talker's Town* and *The Girl Who Swam Forever* – two plays that treat similar issues in entirely different ways – can be part of a much-needed dialogue between First Nations and non-Indigenous people in this country: an example, that is, of how individuals with different histories and world views can address shared concerns in a public space, and be informed by each other's distinctness and difference, in a mutual respectful way.

—NELSON GRAY

AUTHORS' NOTE

These two plays can be read and produced as distinct works or as a pair of plays, treating similar events from different perspectives. When considered in tandem, however, the plays have been designed to begin with *Talker's Town* and to conclude with *The Girl Who Swam Forever*.

Talker's Town

by

NELSON GRAY

PRODUCTION HISTORY

Talker's Town was first produced by Western Edge Theatre in Nanaimo, British Columbia, from January 28 to February 6, 2005, with the following cast and crew:

TALKER	Darren Keltie
RAYMOND-BOB	Bob Chamberlin
ROBERTA-BOB	Kerriann Cardinal
LEROU	Caleb Williamson
GEORGE	Vincent Wells
HARDING	Neil Gallagher
Director	Jessica Lowry
Production Stage Manager	Albert Seibold
Assistant Stage Manager	Katie Hooper
Sound Technician	Bob Chamberlin
Dramaturge	Frank Moher

CHARACTERS

TALKER, middle-aged when narrating the story; fifteen when *in* the story.

Jim "Hard-On" HARDING, sixteen years old.

Gordie LEROU, a tough guy, high school drop-out; works at the mill, twenty years old.

GEORGE McLean, Lerou's buddy, Raymond-Bob and Roberta-Bob's cousin, twenty years old.

ROBERTA-BOB, Indigenous girl, sixteen years old.

RAYMOND-BOB, Roberta-Bob's brother, nineteen years old.

A small mill-town in the Fraser Valley, 1960s.
A chorus of frogs is singing in the April
twilight. Sounds of a sawmill in the distance.
Lights up on TALKER. The other characters
will remain on stage for the duration of the
play, but speaking from the shadows or as
silhouettes behind a scrim, until it's time for
them to play a physical role in the action.

TALKER
When I was a boy I used to climb to the top of the
water tower.

RAYMOND-BOB
The old one, the old water tank, the old wooden
water tank –

ROBERTA-BOB
Yeah, when we were kids we used to climb it –

TALKER
I'd wait till no one was around and sneak into the mill,
making my way between the forklifts and the stacks
of lumber –

LEROU
It was just like climbin' a set o' stairs – it would go this way,
that way, zigzag back and forth –

TALKER
I'd stand at the bottom and look up –

RAYMOND-BOB
  Straight up – that thing musta been about fifty feet high –

TALKER
  I'd keep looking up the whole time I was climbing –

GEORGE
  You look down – you start getting dizzy!

TALKER
  Near the top there was a rickety old wooden platform.
  I'd hold on real tight to those green cedar railings,
  crouch down, lean over, and spit – watching the saliva
  trail and spin –

HARDING
  One, two, three, four – (*counting becoming interspersed with
  TALKER's words*) –

TALKER
  I remember sounds. I remember pictures –

HARDING
  Five, six –

TALKER
  I remember a small town in a big country with an Iroquois
  name and lots of 'A's in it, eh?

HARDING
  Seven, eight –

LEROU
  It was such a nice little town. Everybody knew you when
  you went by –

GEORGE
Mr. Davies had the coffee shop.

ROBERTA-BOB
He used to leave the paper out for the kids every
day – he knew they were coming up –

RAYMOND-BOB
I can remember at one time there was all green trees
around here – I mean it was all bush – all green trees that
the kids used to play around –

LEROU
We lived by the mill whistle. We knew and we always
knew and I know to this day, when I hear so many shoots
on that whistle down there – up until they changed
their system – I knew, when it was four whistles or three
whistles or five whistles, *who was being called* ...

Sound of a long mill whistle blast.

TALKER
I remember a town where the men all smelled like sawdust
and the women washed it out.

ROBERTA-BOB
You couldn't wash it out –

LEROU
That cedar-wood smell –

TALKER
And the smokestack blacks and the wet greens and the
whites across the fields. And the boxcars that went one,
two, three, four, five, six, seven, and the sound of the little

bell at the crossing. And the boys crowing rooster tails into the night: "Hey McKay! Hey Fencepost!"

HARDING
(*really belting it out*) Goose-Pecker! Shiver-Balls!

LEROU and GEORGE respond
with hoots and hollers.

TALKER
And I remember Jim "Hard-On" Harding, walking around the town all night: in the park – by the swings and up on the bleachers – his cuban heels pounding the blacktop pavement – his bow-legged stride on the railway ties, and that high-pitched whistle of his escaping, through cupped hands and finger holes ...

HARDING whistles.

HARDING
Hey, Talker – what's that horrible ugly thing between your legs!

LEROU
Hey Boys! You know what that is, doncha boys!

HARDING
Quick – choke it! Choke the sucker! Kill it before it spreads.

GEORGE
Woo Hoo HOOOO!

TALKER
I remember Jim Harding all right. I remember his
silhouette under the street light, and the rosary as
blue as his eyes when he took it out of his jacket
pocket. I remember thinking, "It looks like a necklace –
a woman's necklace."

HARDING
Horseshit, Talker!

TALKER
Harding?

HARDING
You never climbed no water tower.

TALKER
I did so.

HARDING
When?

TALKER
Last night, around one in the morning – they shut the mill
down early you see and –

LEROU
Oh I don't see how that could be.

RAYMOND-BOB
There was always somebody on shift.

GEORGE
Yeah – the watchman on graveyard woulda seen yas.

HARDING
You and your friggin' stories, Talker!

TALKER
You're interrupting, Harding!

HARDING
I'm *who*?

TALKER
Jim Harding pretty much summed up everything I wanted
to be. Everyone liked him. Even the guys from across
the tracks –

ROBERTA-BOB
The wrong side of the tracks –

TALKER
Guys like Hootchie and Fuzz-Face –

GEORGE
Well, we were river rats, eh?

TALKER
Harding walked down the middle of the street, never on
the sidewalk.

HARDING
Hey boys!

    LEROU and GEORGE hoot back at him.

TALKER
He stayed out until two in the morning.

HARDING
What do you say, eh boys?

LEROU and GEORGE let out a whoop.

TALKER
He could kick ceilings and the tops of doorsills. And he wasn't afraid of anything – not even that old wooden water tower.

HARDING
Come on – what are ya scared of?

TALKER
I can remember Friday nights. All the boys'd be hangin' out on the street, flickin' the boots, hootin' and hollerin' – trying to get a rise out of him –

LEROU and GEORGE
Hey, Hard-On! What the frig you doin'?

HARDING
Hey, boys! Whaddya say, eh boys? It's Friday night, right boys! And we know what that means, don't we boys!

LEROU and GEORGE
Woo Hoo HOOOO!

TALKER
He'd be standing under the street light, that rosary in his jacket pocket, blowing smoke rings into the empty night –

HARDING
One, two, three, four –

TALKER
Perfect circles, linking together to make a chain, and then,
with the flick of a cigarette butt, blowin' 'em all away.

HARDING
Somethin's gonna happen tonight boys. (*"singing" it out*)
I can *FEEL* it!

TALKER
Well, something happened all right. Something weird.

HARDING
Weird?

GEORGE
Nah.

LEROU
No there wasn't much really.

GEORGE
Nothin' that I can recall.

TALKER
Something weird all right. A girl had disappeared,
an Indigenous girl. She'd run away from the Catholic
school, and no one knew where she was hiding.
No one except for me, that is ...

LEROU
Oh sure, Talker.

GEORGE
Yeah, right.

LEROU
Tell us about it, Four-Eyes.

GEORGE
Come on – let's hear it!

LEROU
One of them stories of yours.

LEROU and GEORGE
About the *ba-hooms!*

TALKER
It was six months before my sixteenth birthday,
between the end of March and the beginning of April, that
silhouette time when it's not quite day but not yet night.
The birds had come down early to roost in the trees, and
the steers in the fields were getting frisky – as if something
had spooked them. I was walking along the dike next to
the reserve when all of a sudden, the sky turned ominous –

HARDING
Omni-what?

TALKER
You know, dark clouds and shit. And then the wind
picked up, and the air got cold, and the first few drops
began to fall –

HARDING
One, two, three, four –

TALKER
Spit from the top of the water tower –

RAYMOND and ROBERTA-BOB
(*speaking together*) Green needles falling from giant fir –

HARDING
Oh shit yeah – I remember that storm. Me 'n Goose were
under the bridge, drinkin' his old man's rum –

TALKER
I covered my head with my ski jacket and took off down
this trail –

HARDING
Goose-Pecker was puking his guts out in the river –

TALKER
– overgrown with bushes and blackberry vines –

HARDING
– puke coming out his friggin' nose!

TALKER
Come on, Harding – this is serious!

HARDING
What?

TALKER
I met this girl.

LEROU and GEORGE *murmur and gasp.*

HARDING
Bull twiddy! Where?

TALKER
You're not gonna tell anyone are ya, Jim?

HARDING
Nah.

TALKER
You promise – you swear on your rosary?

HARDING
Talker!

TALKER
Okay, okay – well you know that abandoned fish boat down there?

RAYMOND-BOB
Down by the wharf, eh, where it was beached –

HARDING
That gillnetter – that old rotten rag-picker?

TALKER
Yeah, that's the one. I was heading there to duck outta the rain, see. But as I got closer I could hear this singing …

HARDING
Singing?

TALKER
Yeah!

RAYMOND-BOB
And it was really sad –

ROBERTA-BOB
(*singing the cartoon song from the Huckleberry Hound Dog Show, but in an eerie, sad, minor key*) "Huckleberry Fun is for everyone, for every guy and gal."

TALKER
She was wearing this motorcycle jacket –

ROBERTA-BOB
I used to have this black leather jacket –

TALKER
And bare legs under a flared skirt –

LEROU murmurs approvingly.

ROBERTA-BOB
And crinolines and bobby socks –

HARDING
(*egging him on*) Yeah ... yeah?

TALKER
She had her hands together between her legs –

HARDING
Holy shit!

TALKER
Holding on to something – some kind of charm or something. And she was just sitting there, rocking and singing. And then she started whispering.

ROBERTA-BOB starts softly whispering.

HARDING
Whispering? Whispering what?

TALKER
I couldn't make it out at first, so I crept up closer.

ROBERTA-BOB
Holy Mary Mother of God pray for our sinners now at the
hour of our death pray for our sinners pray for our sinners
pray for our sinners pray for our sinners ...

TALKER
And then I realized I had to go.

HARDING
Go?

TALKER
Yeah, *you know* ...

HARDING
What – take a piss?

TALKER
Yes!

HARDING
You couldn't hold it?

TALKER
Not any more I couldn't! So I put my back to this willow
tree, and crouched down in the weeds, so she wouldn't
see me. But then that stupid thing sprang up, and went up
my pant leg.

HARDING
What were you doin'? Playin' with it?

TALKER
No? What would I do that for?

ROBERTA-BOB
Our parents told us not to touch them – we were told
we'd get warts.

TALKER
Boy, did that ever feel weird though. Big, ugly, slippery
thing – jumping up and down in there, and me dancin'
around like a wild man trying to get rid of the damn
thing … I didn't mean to kill him.

HARDING
Him?

TALKER
It.

ROBERTA-BOB
Chumelah.

HARDING
What the frig!

TALKER
It was an accident! I mean I look up and she's standing
there staring at me with my fly open and everything and
I … Well I just panicked, eh – squeezed too hard –

Sound of a frog croaking.

TALKER
"I'm sorry," I said, "I didn't mean" … I kept waiting for her
to scream. But she didn't. She just stared and stared at it
for what seemed like forever – I didn't mean to kill it.

HARDING
It?

TALKER
The frog.

HARDING
Frog?

TALKER
Yes.

HARDING
(*still trying to put it together*) You killed a frog?

TALKER
Harding! I told you – it was an accident! I thought she
was going to scream or something but she didn't – she just
stood there staring, and then, without saying a word, she
walked over, reached down and took hold of it.

HARDING
The frog?

TALKER
Yes Harding, the frog – the dead frog with its squished-in
head and its gooshy eyeballs hanging out of the sockets!

HARDING
Okay, okay – don't get your shit tied in knots!

TALKER
"I think we should bury it."

HARDING
What?

TALKER
"I think we should bury it" – that's what she said. So we
did. We put it inside this hollowed-out tree stump, and
laid some sticks and moss over it – so the birds wouldn't
peck at it. And then we took shelter inside the old boat
hull, and sat in there together, waiting for the storm
to pass …

HARDING
Un-friggin-believable.

TALKER
I'll say.

HARDING
So who is she anyway?

TALKER
I can't tell you that.

HARDING
Why not?

TALKER
I can't. I gave my word.

HARDING
Oh come on – she's got a name, doesn't she?

TALKER
No – I've said too much already.

HARDING
Holy frig – don't tell me ...

TALKER
What?

HARDING
Did something *happen* between you two?

TALKER
Happen?

HARDING
Yeah, *you know* ...

TALKER
(*drawn into his thoughts for a moment*) It happened Friday
nights at Lerou's house they said that Lerou put a beer
bottle up Mary's skirt and when she said no it's too cold
he just smirked and took out his cigarette lighter and ...
It happened on the dike beside the river and inside the
Valley View Drive-In they said on the walls of the entrance
gate someone had scrawled "Come on in and grease your
pole ..." And I read the writing on the bathroom wall that
said in the bushes behind the pool hall there were –

HARDING
Condoms – lots of them –

TALKER
And under the bleachers –

HARDING
Panties –

TALKER
And Harding said it was happening across the line in dirty
blue movies and magazines in his old man's toolshed and
on Friday nights in town he said if you had the money and
a car ... it was happening *all the time* he said somewhere
he said ... to someone.

HARDING
So?

TALKER
(*snapping out of it*) So ... what?

HARDING
So did something *happen* or didn't it?

TALKER
Well yeah – sort of ...

HARDING
Sort of?

TALKER
But not, *you know* ...

HARDING
Sort of! Hey Boys, listen to this! So what was she,
Talker – a blonde?

TALKER
No – she's ... dark.

HARDING
Oh yeah – a brunette, eh?

TALKER
Yeah, and her skin's kind of brunette too.

HARDING
What – not like no negro or nothin'?

TALKER
No no – nothing like that – no she's more sort of …
Polynesian-looking.

HARDING
Oh yeah, Hawaiian, eh? One of them Hawaiian girls? Like
that one Elvis had in *Blue Hawaii*? Boy, she was nice, eh?
She just had that nice tanned complexion, like Nancy
Ellison – in that classy white bathing suit – down by
Davidson Pool.

> *The Elvis Presley karaoke version*
> *of "Are You Lonesome Tonight" fades*
> *in. We see ROBERTA-BOB, in silhouette,*
> *moving to the music, and, flanked on either*
> *side of her, LEROU and GEORGE, also in*
> *silhouette, playing the part of back-up singers.*

HARDING
(*assuming a dreamy Elvis persona and speaking over the*
music) Are you feeling lonesome tonight? Are you missing
me tonight?

TALKER
Harding?

HARDING
(*drawn out of his Elvis dream*) Shut up, Talker! I wasn't
talking to you. What do you know about Elvis anyway?
You don't know *nothin'* about Elvis!

TALKER
I think I should tell you what really happened –

HARDING
(*Elvis again*) "I wonder if you're lonesome tonight."

TALKER
– down at that old abandoned boat.

HARDING
Somethin's gonna happen tonight, Talker. I can always feel
it when somethin's gonna happen. It's like nothin' happens
and nothin' happens and nothin' happens. And then –

TALKER
– when we were burying that frog –

HARDING
Woo Hoo HOOOO!

TALKER
– our hands came together –

HARDING
(*Elvis again*) "You know someone once said that the
world is a stage, and we each must play a part."

TALKER
Just for a moment, I mean.

HARDING
"Now the stage is bare," and I'm just sorta standin' there.

TALKER
And then she leaned into me, you know, real close, and –

HARDING
(*too excited to keep his cool*) Hey, Crazy Mary – someone popped yer cherry!

TALKER
– and I mean –

HARDING
Don't worry about it, Talker; it's no big deal. She's crazy, for frig's sake. She *lets* them do it. She likes it.

TALKER
It wasn't a kiss or anything.

HARDING
Hey – I said them, not *me* – Jeez what do you take me for? ... "Is your heart filled with pain?" Is it?

TALKER
But as I headed for home that night, I saw the water tower stretching up to the stars, and there you were, Harding –

HARDING
– on that rickety platform –

TALKER
– as if there was nothing to it.

HARDING
Eh, boys?

TALKER
And I felt like I was up there, too: up with the birds
and the plumes of the smokestack, and my head was
spinning around up there, like the merry-go-round
beside the swings, the one with the railings you hold on
to – to keep you from falling – and as I lay awake in my
bed that night, the vines on the wallpaper came to life,
the green shoots spiralling up the bedposts, and winding
around my head like a crown. And I watched the black
cinders from the smokestack falling, lit up by the lights
from the lumber yard, and saw the workers on graveyard
shift, walking ghostly through the fog, and then I heard
it again ... that *sound*, the one she and I had heard that
night, and remembered what she had told me ... about
the old woman in cedar-bark clothing, calling to her, from
under the log booms on the river, and wanting something,
a sacrifice ... and that I wasn't to tell a soul I'd heard it,
and yet I had, I had, I had ... And so, you see, I had to
go back ... I *had* to!

> *Slow fade to a night scene at the abandoned*
> *fish boat down by the river, with a half-*
> *moon peeking through the rain clouds.*

ROBERTA-BOB
(*stepping out from the bushes*) You again? Nobody saw you
come down here, did they?

TALKER
I don't think so.

ROBERTA-BOB
You better hope not.

TALKER
Why?

ROBERTA-BOB
You don't have ears?

TALKER
Pardon?

ROBERTA-BOB
Ears, Mr. Big Nose! I told you. No one can know where I am right now.

TALKER
Why not? Are you in trouble or something?

ROBERTA-BOB
You're the one who could be in trouble – if someone found out you were here with me.

TALKER
Why?

ROBERTA-BOB
Like if my brother Raymond-Bob found out.

TALKER
(getting scared) RAYMOND-BOB? He's your brother?

ROBERTA-BOB
You know what it means to lose someone? To have them just disappear?

TALKER
What do you mean?

ROBERTA-BOB
It happens, you know. Like my grandmother. An accident.
That's what they say. She used to go swimming down
here and – (*hearing something in the bushes*) Shhh!
What was that?

> *The ghostly wail of the mill whistle*
> *blows, followed by conveyor sounds.*

RAYMOND-BOB
Kind of a mournful sound.

TALKER
That's just the mill whistle. It's for the workers on
graveyard shift.

ROBERTA-BOB
That's a good name for it.

TALKER
For what?

ROBERTA-BOB
Your big ears never heard about that, about when they
were digging, down at the mill. George – my cousin –
he was there that night – him and Lerou.

TALKER
Lerou? Gordie Lerou?

> *Lights up on LEROU on smoke break at the Mill.*

LEROU

Well, they had to put a new track in for the pony – the
pony saw. And they had to put a new foundation under it.

*Lights widens to reveal GEORGE, who
has been shovelling sawdust.*

GEORGE

So we got our shovels, the whole works of us – we had to
shovel all this dirt away.

LEROU

Get down about three feet and here was *a skull*. Must have
been an Indian graveyard, a long time ago.

GEORGE

Oh some of the guys were just sick over it. They couldn't –
couldn't work at it – they just threw down their shovels
and walked away … I wouldn't touch the damn thing –
I threw my shovel away, too.

*Light crossfades from LEROU and GEORGE
to ROBERTA-BOB and TALKER.*

ROBERTA-BOB

But the sad thing was, when they were digging down
there – at the mill – the bones they found they didn't …
keep. They just threw them in the river.

A sound in the bushes.

ROBERTA-BOB

(*keeping her voice low*) You better get out of here, Talker.

TALKER
But –

ROBERTA-BOB
Now! Go!

> *TALKER runs off.*

ROBERTA-BOB
(*looking at the river*) So what now, Grandmother? What
do I do now?

> *Another sound in the bushes startles her.*

ROBERTA-BOB
Grandmother?

> *She turns to see HARDING coming out*
> *of the bushes. They gaze at one another*
> *in silence. Slow fade to black.*
> *A long mill whistle blast. Lights up full*
> *on TALKER and HARDING.*

TALKER
(*pacing back and forth*) Shit! Shit! Shit! SHIT!

HARDING
What's with you?

TALKER
You didn't tell anyone did you, Harding?

HARDING
What?

TALKER
About where she was hiding?

HARDING
Why would I?

TALKER
I don't know why the heck I told you!

HARDING
What difference does it make?

TALKER
Because she's gone, that's why! Because I went back to the
boat again this morning and ah shit! Shit! SHIT!

HARDING
Jeezus – will you friggin' cool it!

TALKER
But she told me, Jim! She warned me.

HARDING
Well, what did you expect? She was a runaway, wasn't she?

TALKER
What? What did you say?

HARDING
Oh come on – don't sound so surprised.

TALKER
You *knew* – you knew it was Ray-Bob's sister?

HARDING
Look Dink-Eyes – it wasn't that hard to figure out. The whole bloody town was talking about it.

TALKER
So why didn't you say anything?

HARDING
Why didn't *you*? Everyone's been out lookin' for her – the Catholic school, the parish – and the whole friggin' Indian reserve!

TALKER
But where is she now?

HARDING
How the frig should I know!

TALKER
There's something goin' on, Harding. Something weird.

HARDING
Weird? What do you mean weird?

TALKER
It's what she was trying to tell me. About her grandmother. And now ... ah shit! People are disappearing, Harding – right under our noses!

HARDING
What are you talking about?

TALKER
You heard about Turpington, didn't you?

HARDING
    Well, yeah – that accident.

TALKER
    My uncle told me. He said, the day before it happened,
    he was cutting a twelve-footer, and suddenly all this blood
    started pouring out –

HARDING
    Blood?

TALKER
    – and then he was making another cut and a whole buncha
    salmon swam out.

HARDING
    (*still thinking about the blood*) Jesus.

TALKER
    And then the next night, on graveyard shift, when Gordie
    Lerou was working there –

            The lights fade up on LEROU,
            speaking from the shadows.

LEROU
    Well, they were digging fuel there on the weekends –

TALKER
    – and Turpington was digging away there all by
    himself – just like he always did –

LEROU
    He just had to dig a little more and then ...

TALKER
- and then ...

HARDING
What?

TALKER
Nobody knows for sure – and it's not the first time either –
there's been other guys.

LEROU
Actually, there was two guys, two different fellas.

TALKER
And guess where they found them –

HARDING
Where?

TALKER
Same place they found Turpington –

LEROU
Buried.

TALKER
Under the sawdust.

LEROU
Suffocated.

TALKER
They say maybe there's a ghost in that sawmill. And only
an Indian can get it out.

A ghostly mill whistle blows, mixed
in with an old woman's cry.

TALKER
Shhh! Listen – you hear that?

Voice-over of the Boy from the 1960s film
Invaders from Mars: *"That sound!"*

RAYMOND-BOB
Kind of a mournful sound.

TALKER
It woke me up in my sleep last night –

Voice-over of the Father from Invaders
from Mars: *"Now take it easy, son."*

TALKER
– alien, like the wailing of a ghost, as if someone were
crying out for something, but she didn't know what
she wanted.

HARDING
I don't know what the hell you're talking about – all this
crap about aliens and ghosts and shit!

TALKER
I'm only telling you what I heard.

HARDING
Yeah, well forget it, okay – that's kid's stuff – it's a
buncha hooey!

TALKER
But, Harding, listen – I think something bad has happened. That's why her brother's been acting so weird – beating guys up and everything. It's 'cause he knows something bad has happened to her.

HARDING
(*distracted*) Who?

TALKER
Ray-Bob's sister!

HARDING
So what! She's a friggin' Indian for Chrissake!

> *The sound of Del Shannon's "Runaway" comes blasting out, and the sound of a car pulling over, screeching its tires.*

LEROU
Hey Boys!

> *Sound of two car doors opening and closing.*

HARDING
(*good-naturedly*) Oh oh here comes trouble!

LEROU
Well, holy shit – if it ain't the big Hard-On and his dinky little friend.

HARDING
Lerou, you friggin' animal!

LEROU
An animal? Jeezus, if I'm an animal, what the hell is
George here?

GEORGE *lets out an enormous*
belch, then laughs like a hyena.

LEROU
So what are you boys up to tonight, besides chokin' yer
weasels – or need I ask?

GEORGE *laughs.*

HARDING
Same as you boys, I betcha.

LEROU
Same as *Us*? Jeezus, I didn't think these boys were like that
did you, Georgie?

GEORGE *chuckles fiendishly and*
LEROU *cackles.* TALKER *laughs without*
really knowing what the joke is.

LEROU
What the hell are you laughin' at Four-Eyes? Eh? What do
you know about it?

HARDING
Leave him alone, Lerou – he doesn't know what you're
talking about.

LEROU
Oh but you do, eh Harding?

GEORGE

Yeah – you know *all* about it, don't you, Harding? Shame on you, Hard-On – you bad boy, you!

HARDING

You're crazy, George, you know that – you're a crazy man!

GEORGE

No I'm not. I'm not cra-zee.

LEROU

So did you hear Raymond-Bob's on the warpath?

GEORGE

You should be more *po-lite,* Hard-On – we *know* about you.

LEROU

Watch your mouth, George.

GEORGE

We know, though – don't we, Rou?

LEROU

George!

> *GEORGE laughs his hyena laugh.*

HARDING

So where did you hear that, anyway?

LEROU

What?

HARDING

About Raymond-Bob?

LEROU
   Oh – a little birdie told me. Isn't that right, George? But
   we're not going to let that spoil our weekend, are we?

GEORGE
   Nope!

LEROU
   It's Friday night, (*starting his engine*) right boys? And we
   know what that means, don't we?

GEORGE
   Yeah, Hard-On, we know all right. We *know* all about you!

        GEORGE laughs like a hyena as the
        car roars off down the street.

TALKER
   What was that all about?

HARDING
   Don't worry about it – they were just horsin' around.

TALKER
   That stuff about Raymond-Bob, I mean.

HARDING
   How should I know? I got nothin' to do with it.

TALKER
   You should stay away from him, Jim.

HARDING
   Who?

TALKER
Lerou.

HARDING
Lerou? Nah! He's alright.

TALKER
He knifed that kid from the reserve, remember?

RAYMOND-BOB
We used to break razors and put 'em in ... our shoes ...
in case we got into any fights.

HARDING
So what? Nobody died or nothin'.

TALKER
He took a baseball bat to Terry Adams, broke all his ribs,
and sent him to the hospital.

RAYMOND-BOB
It happened with some of our group, eh – couple of guys
got beat up pretty bad.

TALKER
Raymond-Bob took him on though, didn't he?
Remember that?

RAYMOND-BOB
Well, how it started was at the Twinkle Inn.

HARDING
Ray-Bob and his gang came in for a burger.

TALKER

And Lerou and all his goons are sitting there.

HARDING

Fence post. Creature. The Mackay brothers. The whole bunch of 'em. And they've been drinking, eh?

TALKER

So Lerou, he starts bad-mouthin' Ray-Bob.

LEROU

Hey, you stinkin' Wagon-Burner, who the hell said you could come in here?

HARDING

Well, Ray-Bob isn't going to listen to this, eh?

RAYMOND-BOB

Up yours, White-Ass!

TALKER

Pretty soon everyone was crowdin' around.

GEORGE

Forming a circle.

HARDING

Yelling – goading them on.

TALKER

Everybody knew Lerou's reputation.

HARDING

We all figured the Indian kid would back down.

TALKER
He didn't though.

GEORGE
They squared off. Couple a pushes, couple a shoves.
That was it.

TALKER
I couldn't believe it. Lerou. Gordie Lerou backing down
from a fight!

HARDING
Yeah. And then that stupid little Dodson kid: "Come on
Lerou, you're not gonna take that are ya?"

A cymbal crashes with rapid snare drum
solo throughout the following monologue.

TALKER
(*speaking throughout, his memories of LEROU's*
assault intercut with memories of song titles, lyrics, and
sound bites from the era) I remember Lerou's boots
comin' up fast and hard – "Come on baby, let's do
the twist" – and Dodson lying white-faced in the
dust – "Wise men say only fools rush in" – his balls
crushed his – "Mashed potatoes" – mouth bleeding –
"It's a bird … It's a plane" – no it's – "The majestic, the
majestic" – Harding just standing there laughing
and – "Yes I'm the great pretender" – afraid to say what
I really think – "Superman" – ? And walking silently
away – now "I'm the type of guy that likes to roam around"
(*cymbal crash*) – Why?

Lights dim. Sound of a chorus of frogs begins
to fade up from under the seats of the audience.

RAYMOND-BOB and ROBERTA-BOB
are watching the boys from the shadows.
HARDING croaks like a bullfrog.

TALKER
(*whispering*) Jim?

Sound of a big bullfrog croak.

HARDING
Shhh!

TALKER
What are ya doin?

HARDING croaks again.

TALKER
You can't just talk to 'em like that.

ROBERTA-BOB
Chumelah.

HARDING
Why not?

TALKER
They won't understand you.

RAYMOND-BOB
Chumelah.

HARDING
Why not? (*turning his flashlight on a member of the audience*) Look. There's one of 'em over there.

TALKER
Yeah, a big one!

HARDING
Ugly! (*lighting up another audience member*) And there's
another one. See!

TALKER
(*sweeping his flashlight over a number of faces*) Yeah – holy
shoot – there's a whole bunch of 'em.

HARDING
Look at 'em all – just sittin' there, with their little pokey-
out eyes buggin' out.

TALKER
What do you think they're doin'?

HARDING
(*creeping up on the audience*) I dunno – let's find out.
Shhh! Come on ...

> *Sound of a big bullfrog croak from*
> *behind the boys, startling them.*

HARDING
(*turning his flashlight on it*) Hey you! Green head!
What's up? Yes you, buddy – wake up, I'm talking
to you! What are you, deaf or something?

> *All the frogs are silent now. Pause. Then from*
> *another direction, another brave bullfrog croaks.*

HARDING
Hey, you! Frog-Face! You got something to say, Web-Foot?
Come on! SPIT IT OUT!

TALKER
(*joining in and getting carried away*) Yeah, you heard
him – buddy! That's right – you heard what he said! Yeah.
Alright. Party time. Woo-hoooo! Juicy-Lucy! (*realizing he's
all on his own now*) Yeah ... Alright...
I ... ah ... um ... (*pause*)

HARDING
I think you scared 'em.

TALKER
Yeah.

HARDING
Too bad.

TALKER
Yeah.

HARDING
I like frogs.

TALKER
Me, too.

HARDING
Ever get scared?

TALKER
No. You?

HARDING
Nah. (*pause*) What scares ya?

TALKER
Me? What scares me? ... Eyes. Eyes in the dark. Staring at me. Animals.

> *Lights dim to a night scene. Frog sounds become more menacing now, transformed into a rhythmic, ritualistic pulsing and thrumming, like the sound of a bullroarer. In the darkness, TALKER and HARDING use their flashlights to light objects, their faces, and one another.*

TALKER
Hey – remember when Cathy Morrison's mom died and she started growing her fingernails really long? ... Well last night she got drunk at the prom dance. And they said that later that night, she took off her white dress, burnt it, and threw the ashes into the slough!

HARDING
Weird!

> *A lighter flicks on, the flame warming up a beer bottle, then, just as suddenly, flicks shut.*

TALKER
Yeah! – And then yesterday, Raymond-Bob, who's always so quiet in history class – all of a sudden, at lunch, he's standing outside the school exit doors, and when any of the guys tried to leave, he starts punchin' them – right in the head!

> *Sound of a whip crack.*

HARDING
Who's that? Is someone there?

TALKER
Harding, remember you told me those stories about
Lerou's house. Well, lately I've been hearing sounds
comin' from there – really weird sounds. And the other
morning at school they heard this weird singing, and they
found Crazy Mary sitting in the fire escape, with her skirt
torn, just rocking and singing – "Huckleberry Fun is for
everyone" – and she had teeth marks on her legs!

   Sound of a dog snarl.

TALKER
Lerou?

   The lights come up downstage on the two boys.
   Behind them are the silhouettes of two teenaged
   girls, swaying their hips to music. HARDING
   is staring straight ahead, as if seeing the girls in
   front of him. TALKER is using his flashlight
   to learn about sex by reading a dictionary.

HARDING
Holy shit! – It's Nancy Ellison, the Alderman's daughter,
and whatshername, you know, the ugly one – the one you
like. (*channelling Elvis again*) "It's time I started doing
something for myself for a change, like making my own
decisions." Hi Nancy. (*after getting no response*) Nance?

   Sound of canned laughter.

HARDING

(*as Elvis*) "What if she doesn't like me? I don't want to
listen to that kind of talk. I don't want to listen to that ..."
Come on, Talker – you're the one with the big words – say
something, for frig's sake!

TALKER

(*reading his dictionary*) Break. Breaking Point. *Breast.*
"Noun. Anat. The outer front part of the thorax, or the
front part of ..." Vain. Vague. *Vagina.* "The passage leading
from the uterus to the vulva. Cf. *oviduct.*" Oviduct?

> *Sound of the mill whistle again, followed by silence.*
> *Then a voice-over of LEROU, singing in falsetto,*
> *the lyrics from the Lesley Gore song "She's a Fool."*

LEROU

"She don't know that she's a lucky girl."

HARDING

(*as the lights go down on the silhouettes of the two girls*)
Nancy? Nance?

> *Nancy pauses, looks back at HARDING, and exits.*

Hey, wait – where are you goin'?

LEROU

(*singing, voice-over*) "Got the best thing in the whole
wide world."

HARDING

(*responding to Nancy's departure*) Okay, fine
then – be a snob!

*The lights fade up from behind the
scrim to reveal, very dimly, the images
of ROBERTA-BOB and LEROU.*

LEROU and ROBERTA-BOB
(*singing together as the lights fade out*) "Got a love that's
hard to find."

HARDING
(*still talking to the absent Nancy*) What – have I got the
clap or something?

TALKER
Harding? Harding – listen to me, there's something else,
something I haven't told you – but you gotta swear this
time, you gotta swear you won't say a word about this –
not to anyone.

HARDING
Swear? For what?

TALKER
On your rosary.

HARDING
Why?

TALKER
Because if Lerou ever finds out about this I could
be in deep –

HARDING
Shit!

TALKER
What?

HARDING
Where is it?

TALKER
What?

HARDING
My rosary – what the frig!

TALKER
It's not in your pocket?

HARDING
No.

TALKER
When did you last have it?

HARDING
I don't know – last night I guess – I – ah, frig – what the
hell is goin' on!

TALKER
I don't know, Harding – things just keep getting weirder
and weirder. And that's not all either! You see when she
didn't show up at the boat this morning, I got on my bike
and went looking for her everywhere: the pool hall, the
park, the drugstore. And then, when I was riding home,
I passed by Gordie Lerou's house ...

RAYMOND-BOB
It was just a little old dirty old house – but it had a
reputation –

HARDING
(*remembering*) Lerou's house – of course!

TALKER
And I heard these weird sounds comin' from there.

*Sound of drunken singing and
laughter:"Huckleberry Fun is for
everyone – every guy and gal."*

HARDING
At that stupid party.

TALKER
And then there was this moaning sound, like someone was
in pain or something –

HARDING
Let's hitch a ride outa here, Talker.

TALKER
What do you mean?

HARDING
(*stepping into the shadows*) Come on, stick
your thumb out.

TALKER
No – listen to me, Harding! It was her, I'm sure of it!
I got on my bike and rode up the sidewalk to the front

door, but then these sharp white teeth lunged out of
the bushes –

Sound of a dog snarl.

TALKER

– and sent my bike flying into the ditch. Inside, I could
hear laughter. And then the door opened, and Lerou
stepped out, and behind me –

*Sound of a dog growl and GEORGE's
mad hyena laughter.*

TALKER

– I bolted. I ran home, locked the front door, and sat there
staring at the TV. Aliens! A boy was watching a flying
saucer blasting a hole in the ground with its ray gun, and
disappearing into the earth.

Voice-over of the Father from Invaders from
Mars: *"Now look son, you were dreaming."*

TALKER

And then the earth swallowed up his parents –

Voice-over of the Boy from Invaders
from Mars: *"Mom! Dad!"*

TALKER

– and they became aliens too.

Voice-over of the Father from Invaders from
Mars: *"Now you listen to me, we don't want you
telling a lot of those idiotic stories you understand?"*

TALKER
And he was running through the main street of town,
pounding on screen doors, and banging on windows – the
barber shop, the gas station –

Voice-over of the Boy from Invaders from
Mars: *"Please Jim, you gotta believe me."*

TALKER
– but noone in the town would believe him, because he
was the only one who could hear it.

Voice-over of the Boy from Invaders
from Mars: *"That sound!"*
Sound of dialing of an old rotary telephone.

TALKER
Hello! Police!

Voice-over of the Boy from Invaders
from Mars: *"Is this the Chief?"*

TALKER
Something bad is happening at Lerou's house.

GEORGE
(*Voice-over*) We was forever bein' raided.

TALKER
But they didn't find anything. And later, when I went back
for my bike –

LEROU
(*Voice-over*) You may as well kiss it goodbye, Talker. I just
saw Raymond-Bob riding away on it. And he was going
like hell toward the river.

RAYMOND-BOB
(*Voice-over*) I used to get accused all the time of throwing
bikes into the river.

TALKER
Raymond-Bob? Are you sure?

LEROU
(*Voice-over*) Well, who else would it be, Jelly-Balls?

TALKER
(*back to the present and suddenly alone*) But I don't think it
was Raymond-Bob, Jim.

> *The sound of a car pulling over. Headlights*
> *on TALKER – and on HARDING,*
> *who has had his thumb out.*

HARDING
Hey, Talker – we're in luck!

TALKER
Harding! What did you do that for?

HARDING
I got us a ride. Come on!

> *Car doors open and shut. LEROU and*
> *GEORGE step into the headlights.*

TALKER
(*hanging back*) Oh – I don't know, Jim. I sort of feel like walking tonight.

LEROU
I wouldn't do that if I were you. Not with Raymond-Bob on the loose.

GEORGE
Yeah – he catches you out here – you could lose more than your bike.

HARDING
He's tellin' the truth, Talker.

LEROU
Make up your mind, boys!

> *Everybody piles in but TALKER.*
> *LEROU fires up the engine.*

HARDING
(*opening the car door*) Come on – hop in!

> *TALKER climbs in.*

LEROU
(*starting off*) All right – that's more like it!

HARDING
So what are you guys drinking tonight?

LEROU
(*opening a beer*) Oh you know us, Hard-On. We don't drink, do we George?

GEORGE
    Nope. (*opening a beer*) That's for bad boys, right Rou?
    (*loud belch*)

HARDING
    Can you guys get us some?

LEROU
    Jeezus, I dunno – we could get into trouble
    supplying to minors.

LEROU
    Yeah, like last time, eh?

LEROU
    George!

HARDING
    Come on, George – gimme a beer.

LEROU
    Pull his hair and he'll give you one.

HARDING
    Frig you!

LEROU
    Go ahead – he likes it! Don't ya, Georgie? Watch!

        GEORGE pulls his own hair, makes a
        face, and laughs like a madman.

HARDING
    You guys are friggin' crazy!

GEORGE
(*handing HARDING a bottle of wine*) I'm not – hehehaha!
I am not cra-zee – ha ha ha!

> *LEROU and GEORGE roar with laughter.*

LEROU
Drink up, boys!

TALKER
(*speaking over the sound of the engine*) Everything spinning
outside the car window – trees, telephone poles –

HARDING
Where the hell are you takin' us, Lerou?

TALKER
Everything swilling and swirling around.

LEROU
Jeezus, I dunno George, where're we goin?

> *GEORGE laughs like a hyena.*

TALKER
The river!

LEROU
(*coming to a stop and turning the engine off*) This is as far as
we go boys.

TALKER
A big sign nailed to an alder tree: "Indian Reserve."

LEROU
The ol' drinkin' hole.

TALKER
"Trespassers Keep Out."

GEORGE
Something the matter, Tal-ker?

TALKER
I think I'm gonna be sick.

GEORGE laughs.

HARDING
What is this stuff anyway?

LEROU
Cherry wine, boys!

HARDING
Yeah, well, how come you guys aren't drinking it?

GEORGE
We go back on graveyard tonight that's why.

LEROU
That's right – ya don't expect us to go into work all
shitfaced, do yas?

TALKER
Graveyard?

LEROU

That's right, Pecker-Head, some guys gotta work for a
living – unlike some little boys I know. Besides, ain't you
heard yet – I got promoted. I'm in the power house now!

TALKER

(*to HARDING, keeping his voice down*)
Turpington's old job.

LEROU

Yeah, that's right. Turpentine's job. What about it?

HARDING

Talker figures there was somethin' behind it –
that accident.

TALKER

Harding!

HARDING

Somethin' weird.

LEROU

Oh he does, does he?

TALKER

No – I never meant –

LEROU

You never meant, you never mean, but you do anyway,
don't you, Shiver Shit! Blah, blah, blah – tongue wagging
around all the time, spreadin' stories behind people's
backs. You keep that shit up, you're gonna lose it one of
these days. Someone might come along and cut the sucker
out – then what would you do, eh? Then what would you

say, Diarrhea Mouth? Not very much, would ya! (*long pause; silence all around*) Well – what a night, eh? Jesus, I love this place. The river. The stars. Fuckin' stars, eh? Pretty quiet tonight, aren't they? ... Don't have a fuck of a lot to say, I guess.

A sound in the bushes.

HARDING
What was that?

LEROU
Where?

TALKER
Someone's out there!

LEROU
What are you talking about? All it is is the goddamn –

Someone farts.

HARDING
Oh crap – who cut the cheese?

LEROU
Harding – Jeezus!

HARDING
It wasn't me – it was George!

LEROU
George! Holy shit, do you stink!

GEORGE farts.

LEROU
George!

GEORGE laughs.

HARDING
Holy frig – lemme outta here!

Sound of a car door opening and shutting.

LEROU
Where the hell is he goin'?

GEORGE
(*laughing*) He's taking a leak.

LEROU
Him and his little friend.

GEORGE
No Four-Eyes is passed out already.

LEROU
Off in dreamland.

GEORGE
Saw-ing logs!

TALKER
(*whispering*) But I wasn't. I was listening.

GEORGE
So what happens now, Rou?

LEROU
What do you mean?

GEORGE
If people start finding out I mean.

LEROU
Well, that's not our problem, is it? Besides, this kinda thing
happens all the time. You watch, in a little while, it'll be
like nothin' ever happened.

GEORGE
What about Four-Eyes, though?

LEROU
What about him?

GEORGE
What if he starts tellin' stories?

LEROU
Nobody's gonna believe him, Georgie.

GEORGE
Raymond-Bob might.

LEROU
Well, that would be different, wouldn't it? I mean, that
would be crossing a line.

Sound of a whistle blast from an approaching train.

HARDING
Hey boys! You hear that, boys?

TALKER
I heard it all right.

HARDING
It's a friggin' train, boys!

TALKER
And it was like a spike went through my brain.

LEROU
Alright, boys – let's race it! Let's race the train!

TALKER
No! Don't! Lemme out!

GEORGE
Oh no you don't, Four-Eyes!

Sound of a train whistle.

LEROU
Here she comes, boys!

GEORGE
Get in the car, Harding!

*Sound of another train blast
from the other direction.*

HARDING
Holy shit – another one!

GEORGE
Ya hear that, Lerou – there's two of 'em comin'!

HARDING
Two trains, boys!

LEROU
(*starting the car*) Let's go!

TALKER
No – don't! Don't be crazy!

GEORGE
We'll see who's crazy!

TALKER
The headlights flashed out across the river –

HARDING
Two trains, boys – we're threading the needle.

TALKER
And then I saw it.

GEORGE
Holy shit!

HARDING
Woo Hoo HOOOO!

TALKER
On the log booms.

HARDING
On the ba-hoooms, boys!

TALKER
A shape –

GEORGE
  On the ba-hooms!

TALKER
  Shut up, Harding!

LEROU
  The ba-hooms? – What?

GEORGE
  He saaaaaw something –

LEROU
  Who did?

HARDING
  Taalker – He saaaaw something!

GEORGE and HARDING
  On the ba-HOOMS!

> *Sound of a train whistle practically*
> *right on top of them.*

TALKER
  Wait! Stop!

LEROU
  You wouldn't go blabbing to Raymond-Bob, would you?

TALKER
  No – don't!

GEORGE
  One night the guy didn't stop –

HARDING
Holy shit!

GEORGE
He tried to outrun that train and –

LEROU
You're not an Indian lover, are ya?

TALKER
Look out! STOP!

HARDING
(*with ROBERTA-BOB, in a voice-over*) Holy Mary mother of God pray for your sinners, pray for your sinners, pray for your sinners, PRAY FOR YOUR SINNERS! ...

LEROU
SAY YOUR HAIL MARYS, BOYS!

> *Sound of the crossing bell clanging,*
> *followed by absolute silence.*

GEORGE
Yeah, that old track. I've seen quite a few people killed. One of my best friends lost his leg.

> *Sound of a loud train whistle. Rush*
> *of the passing train.*

HARDING
(*with LEROU and GEORGE hooting and hollering*) Ho-ly shit!

LEROU
We friggin' made it, boys!

GEORGE
You could feel the wind; we were that close.

HARDING
Woo Hoo HOOOO!

GEORGE
Damn near got killed!

LEROU
Hahahahahahah!

TALKER
I'm getting outta here!

LEROU
What for?

HARDING
He thinks he saw something.

GEORGE
On the ba-hooms!

LEROU
On the ba-hooms, eh? Maybe you better go with
him, Harding.

HARDING
Are you sure? You guys gonna wait for us?

LEROU
  Sure. We're not goin' anywhere, are we George?

GEORGE
  Nope!

HARDING
  Alright – we'll be right back.

> As soon as HARDING is out of
> the car, LEROU steps on it.

LEROU
  See you later, boys!

> LEROU and GEORGE howl with
> laughter as the car roars away.

GEORGE
  (*yelling out the window*) Let us know if you find anything!

HARDING
  Assholes! Ah frig – there goes our bloody ride!

TALKER
  So what, Harding – I saw something back there! A body or
  something, I'm sure of it.

HARDING
  (*taking off*) Yeah, well you can go check it out if you want.
  I'm going to Lerou's place to get us some alcohol.

TALKER
  (*calling after him*) Lerou's place? But Harding, you should
  have heard what they said back there – Harding? Harding?

(*really alone now*) You know something, Jim – when I get a car, we're gonna go places together. We'll drive to Hope and come back the same night. We'll go to Cultus Lake with girls we've never met and stop at the gas station and fill 'er up, and there will be enough gas to take us to Mexico if we want, enough to take us anywhere. And we'll step on it and step on it. We'll put our feet to the floor, pedal to the metal, and it'll be passing gear forever. And we'll have beer in the backseat or a mickey and it'll all be completely legal. And we'll go as fast as we want without getting into any accidents ... And we won't kill any Indian girls ... And time will unthaw like the winter ... (*pause*) And neither one of us will go to university or steal cars or work at the mill. We'll just keep on driving toward no-end-in-sight. And the windshield wipers will wipe away rain, not tears. And there will be no blood on the hood ornament, or shattered glass, or fists pounding the gravel. 'Cause it will always be sunset and sunrise, and we'll be just pulling out onto that smooth, smooth pavement. And it will always be just –

RAYMOND-BOB
Looking for something, Talker?

TALKER
Raymond-Bob?

RAYMOND-BOB
Lost something? (*pause*) Someone steal it? Is that it? (*pause*) Maybe that explains what you're doing around here, poking your nose around like a mole, messin' in things that are none of your business.

TALKER
I – I thought I saw something out there, on the log booms.

RAYMOND-BOB
An otter maybe – or a beaver.

TALKER
No it was something else – if we could get out there I
could show you.

RAYMOND-BOB
I don't think so, Talker. Too dangerous –
especially at night.

TALKER
But –

RAYMOND-BOB
Something might happen to you out there. Big sturgeon
come up and get ya. You could slip, lose your balance, get
sucked underneath. Then what would you do? 'Cause the
booms are so tight together. You don't know what's under
there, either.

TALKER
But you don't understand, I saw –

RAYMOND-BOB
(*interrupting*) No – you don't understand. And you wanna
know why? It's 'cause you don't belong here, that's why.
So why don't you just clear out and go home.

TALKER
I would but ... it's a long way and ... I lost my bike.

RAYMOND-BOB
Your bike, eh?

TALKER
Yeah, last night – at Lerou's place.

RAYMOND-BOB
And what does that have to do with me?

TALKER
Nothing – I mean, I was just wondering, what do you think happened to it? (*pause*)

RAYMOND-BOB
I don't know, Talker – why don't you tell me?

TALKER
He said it was you.

RAYMOND-BOB
What?

TALKER
Lerou. He said you threw it in the river.

RAYMOND-BOB
It?

TALKER
My bike ... But, but – I didn't believe him, see, because ... well, I'm pretty sure it was him that did it, and ... and ...

RAYMOND-BOB
And *what*?

TALKER

And that's what I've been trying to tell you, Ray-Bob,
'cause I'm afraid, see, I'm afraid that … that it's the same
with your sister.

RAYMOND-BOB quickly turns to go.

TALKER

Raymond-Bob – wait! Where are you going?

RAYMOND-BOB

You've said enough, Talker.

TALKER

But –

RAYMOND-BOB

Oh and come to think of it – maybe I did see your
bike today.

TALKER

Where?

RAYMOND-BOB

Not too far from here, there's an old rotten gillnetter,
used to belong to my uncle. I'm pretty sure I seen a bike
around there.

*RAYMOND-BOB exits. Lights cross-
fade to the abandoned boat hull.*

TALKER

By the time I got there it was nearly midnight. A sliver of
moonlight had pierced the rain clouds, lighting up that
hollowed stump where she and I had made that little

frog grave. The moss shimmered. Silver. White. Like
the wool from a goat. Incandescent. I moved the sticks
and dirt away, but there were no bones, nothing, not a
trace. I looked everywhere for my bike. Not a sign of it.
And then the sky pulled in all around, and a dampness
gathered. I ducked back into that mouldy old carcass of
a boat, pulled my jacket over my head, crunched myself
into a little ball, and with my head tucked in between my
knees, I began to rock, back and forth, back and forth,
back and forth ...

HARDING
(*with a creepy sing-song refrain*) "Huckleberry Fun is
for everyone."

TALKER
Jim? Is that you?

HARDING
You're dreaming, Talker. You're having a dream – and it's
the same one you've been havin' for years. You're lying
out on the log booms, being carried down by the current.
And then, from down below, something rises and breaks
through the surface of the water. Something old and scaly.
It's been sleeping in the mud, and you've woken it. And
when you look back to shore, you see more of them –
sturgeons, Talker – hundreds of 'em, on the river bank,
suffocating, drowning in air.

TALKER
(*talking in his sleep*) No! Help! Somebody! Please!

HARDING
Oh come on – what's wrong? You're not afraid of your
own story, are yas?

TALKER

(*continuing to talk in his sleep*) No – don't!

HARDING

Yeah, you're scared all right. Ha! Ha! Practically
pissin' yourself!

TALKER

So what, Harding? Maybe there's a reason for it.

HARDING

Nah – it's just a story, for frig's sake!

TALKER

Okay, big shot. You think you're so smart? You tell it then.

HARDING

Me?

TALKER

Sure. What's wrong? Cat got your tongue? Go ahead,
finish it. Finish the story!

HARDING

Well, I dunno, I mean, I'm not usually too big on words,
eh, but, ah – okay, so ... So there you are, eh – snoring
away in that stinkin' old fishboat, off in dreamland – and
then ... You roll over, open your eyes, and – HOLY FRIG!
You're lookin straight down – fifty feet or more! Well you
just about friggin' wet yourself, eh? Hands grabbing for
the cedar railings. And then you get up – tremblin' – tryin'
not to look down. Your knees are shakin'. Your throat's dry.
And the friggin' sky is circling around like a bloody merry-
go-round. And no horizon, eh? Just this deep, dizzying
blue goin' on for friggin' ever. And down below, on the

log booms in the river – there she is, Talker. Ray-Bob's sister. And she's wearing this skimpy white bathing suit, and clutching this rosary between her long, beautiful legs. And she's calling to you, Talker. Oh Talker! Taaalker!

TALKER
Stop it – what are you doing?

HARDING
Ha ha! Pretty good, eh? So then ... There's this big blue heron, eh – a big sucker – and it goes glidin' past, stretching its big grey feathery wings out and soaring way up high above the water. And I'm standing on the bird's back and ... And then I take a big deep breath and whoosh! I'm taking the big dive, right? Arms, chest and legs outstretched in a perfect five-point, and then, tucking in at the waist, I jackknife into a one-eighty and drop straight as a plumb line into the water, piercing it like a needle, and scrambling up the river bank, barking like a friggin' sea lion. *Ouw! Ouw! Ouw! Ouw! Ouw!* ... And now it's your turn Talker. Ray-Bob's sister – she's down there, wavin' to ya, eggin' ya on – "Come on baby. Come to Mama!" But then that shaky old platform below you gives way, and holy frig you're falling! You twist, trying to regain your balance, hitting the water in a half dive, half belly flop. OOOOOH! You try to surface, eh, but you can't – 'cause something wraps around your ankle – something weird and slimy. Alien. And now you're trapped down there, under the booms, and the current's got ya ... So you see she was right, Talker. There's something under there all right. Down there with the rusted barbed wire and old junker car parts, beneath the sawdust and sunken cedar chips –

TALKER
(*still in his sleep*) Tangled lines, drowned speech –

HARDING

Somethin' alien – waiting to sing – how long can ya hold
your breath, Talker? You might've started like a little
tadpole, but you got lungs now. You can't breathe water
like a slippery fish no more. Just like them frogs that bury
themselves in the mud – you're gonna have to come
up sometime!

> *ROBERTA-BOB appears from the*
> *bushes with TALKER's bike.*

ROBERTA-BOB

I thought you had ears, Mr. Big Nose. I told you not to
come back here, remember?

> *ROBERTA-BOB sets the bike down and exits with*
> *HARDING. The sound of frogs. Cross-fade to pre-*
> *dawn morning. Sound of a long slow mill whistle.*

TALKER

(*waking up*) My bike! Had it been there all along?
Or had she come back to give it to me. Rescued it from
the bottom of the river and surfaced on its spinning
wheels? Either way, I had it back at last, and I could go
home. Home! I could go home, and this would all be over.
But, then, as I was pedalling past the cedar mill, I saw
the log booms hauled up from the river, and they were
heading for the trim saw … So I'm standing outside the
mill yard, feeling the ground shake, looking for a way in
through the dry kilns, climbing into the crawl space below
the whirling blade of the head rig –

GEORGE

– a blade – ten, maybe twelve feet long.

TALKER
– and another saw, above and to the left –

LEROU
– the number three saw – the trimmer –

TALKER
– its teeth tearing the cellulose fibre, sawdust spraying like
rooster tails. Gears – moving conveyors –

GEORGE
– you coulda got caught on a chain, you coulda got
caught on a belt –

TALKER
And there – below the slashers, the trimmers, the slab
chains, I see something, half buried in bark and cedar
chips: a skirt? a crinoline? the ragged sleeve of a black
leather jacket? I can't be sure. I reach out, stretching my
hand across the conveyor. Almost. I've almost got it. And
then I feel these stumps at the back of my neck –

LEROU
(*hauling* TALKER *out of the sawdust*) Jeezus, was that ever
friggin' close!

TALKER
Lerou!

LEROU
You trying to get yourself killed, Talker?

TALKER
No – please.

LEROU

Please? Please? (*holding up the stumps of his right hand*)
You see these, Talker? That's right – take a real long good
look. Cause I didn't always have these stumps, see? I used
to have eight, nice, pretty, pink fingers – just like yours.
But last winter I was working in the shingle mill, and
something happened, eh?

TALKER

Happened?

LEROU

Well it was one of them nights when there was more
ice than there was wood. And I put a block on the
machine – and all the bark and the ice fell down,
on the floor –

GEORGE

It didn't take much – a coupla seconds, that's all.

LEROU

I had two shingles in my hand, I went to kick it down the
hole and I slipped on it – zoooooom – head first for the
clipper saw.

GEORGE

For a moment there, he was starin' right at it –

LEROU

So I put my hand up, to *save* my FACE, eh? And my arm
came down on the guard, and knocked my hand down
in the saw.

GEORGE

But he was lucky, eh – 'cause it taught him a lesson.

LEROU

Oh I didn't want twice – no. I didn't want to do that twice. Now you think about that when you're tellin' those stories of yours. You start gettin' careless, makin' mistakes – things happen. Accidents. Stuff you never intended. Now you think about that real good, Talker, you hear?

GEORGE

'Cause all it takes is one zip and it's gone.

LEROU

Here, take this pitchfork. I got a real good job for ya. You see down in there?

TALKER

That was the "Dark Hole"!

LEROU

Go on, you jump down in there with me. That's right – now start digging. No not like that – like this!

> *LEROU grabs the fork and starts digging*
> *through the sawdust, then stops and*
> *hands the fork back to TALKER.*

LEROU

So you wanna know who got that Indian girl pregnant?

TALKER

Pregnant?

LEROU

Why don't you get your friend Harding to tell you?

TALKER
Harding? What are you talking about?

LEROU
Accidents happen, Talker. He got careless is all. Not much
of a story, eh? (*pause*) Oh – and when you see him again –
you might want to give him this. (*tossing him a rosary*)
I found it under the bed this morning, when Raymond-
Bob came around asking questions. Your friend will be
wanting to say a few Hail Marys – now that the cat's outta
the bag. Now, go on, get outta here – and if you know
what's good for yas, don't ever come back.

> *Sound of a saw blade making a cut on a
> timber. Lights cross-fade to HARDING,
> having a smoke at the base of the water tower.
> TALKER runs in, holding the rosary.*

TALKER
Liar! Liar! You stupid liar!

HARDING
What the frig ...?

TALKER
You were there, Harding! You were there that night!

HARDING
I – *what*?

TALKER
At Lerou's place! You lost something there – remember?
(*holding up the rosary*)

HARDING
Where did you get that?

TALKER
(*interrupting*) Go ahead, Harding – shrug it off! Make
a joke of it! Tell me I'm crazy. That this isn't yours. That
Raymond-Bob stole yours and threw it in the river!

HARDING
What the frig are you talking about?

TALKER
That's right – deny it! Tell me it's not what it seems, say
it's a string of petrified frog eggs – or a necklace made of
Indian beads.

HARDING
I don't have to listen to this crap.

TALKER
Come on, Harding. Tell me a story. Make me believe!
(*pause, then to the audience*) But he didn't. He didn't say
anything. He just looked at those blue beads like they
were alive, like they were someone's eyes looking back at
him, piercing him … (*pause, then to HARDING*) What's
the matter, Harding – don't you want it?

HARDING
Nah – you found it. It's yours. Keep it!

TALKER
What happened that night, Harding?

HARDING
None of your friggin' business.

TALKER
Come on – I was outside, remember. I *heard* her.

HARDING
You heard? You heard? You don't know what you heard.
You don't have a friggin' clue.

TALKER
Oh yes I do, Harding. Lerou told me.

HARDING
He *what?*

TALKER
You *lied* to me, Harding!

HARDING
No Talker. You're the liar. Going around saying things –
telling everybody you climbed that water tower. What a
friggin' pile of crap. You never had the guts. But I do!

TALKER
I watched him turn and start to climb. He was right, I'd
cried wolf too many times, bragged about things I never
did. This time it was going to be different. My hands
reached out for the ladder, my fingers holding on tight to
the rungs – one, two, three, four –

HARDING
What the frig do you think you're doing?

TALKER
Five, six – below me I could hear conveyors moving.
Fingers lopped off from sawyer's hands were reaching up
to grab my neck. Six, seven, eight, nine –

HARDING
Get down, for frig's sake!

TALKER
Sweat dripping from beards and foreheads. Clogged lungs.
Severed arms. A lost glass eye, kicked back from
the chipper, watched me climbing step by step. Eleven,
twelve ... tell me the truth, Harding!

HARDING
Are you crazy? You want us both to fall?

TALKER
The truth! (*to the audience*) Below me the ground began
to rise up. Bones rising up from the river, up from the
bark and the cedar sawdust, and a hand – a hand that had
come alive – grabbing my pant leg.

RAYMOND-BOB
Get out of my way, Talker.

TALKER
Raymond-Bob!

ROBERTA-BOB
(*echoing TALKER from the base of the tower*) Ray – don't!

LEROU
What the hell's goin' on up there!

HARDING
Be careful, for Christ's sake.

RAYMOND-BOB
You're the one shoulda been more careful!

ROBERTA-BOB
No – don't.

GEORGE
Raymond-Bob – watch out!

LEROU and GEORGE
(*overlapping*) Look out!

TALKER
What happened then? I don't remember. All I know is that
we were falling. Falling and falling in a dream of falling.

RAYMOND-BOB
I fell for about six weeks or so.

TALKER
And all the stories of the town fell with us.

ROBERTA-BOB
My father used to have a job ringing the light bell.

TALKER
Spit from the top of the water tower …

GEORGE
(*correcting ROBERTA-BOB*) The light bell (*little laugh*) –
the death bell, you mean.

TALKER
Scattering into random patterns …

ROBERTA-BOB
And all the time, day and night, he'd be up there ringing
the death bell.

TALKER

I lay there, eyes closed, not moving. Going over all the
parts of my body: arms, legs, hands, fingers. Nothing
broken. Nothing missing. A pile of sawdust had broken
my fall, with Raymond-Bob lying safely beside me. But
Harding ... Jim Harding hadn't been so lucky. (*pause*)
Something had happened all right. An accident. A sacrifice.
And did I hear, in the clanging of boxcars and mill yard
machinery, the sound of an old woman's voice crying
out, in the squealing of gulls and empty conveyors and
the gang saws spinning the sky around? (*pause*) And a
long black car, its tires crushing the gravel. A window
wound down, a white face twitched. Words, aliens,
invaded my body.

LEROU

You and your friggin' stories, Talker!

TALKER

The sky wheeled. The ground spun around. I took hold of
what he had given to me, clutched it like shame, like pride,
like a curse and a crime, and I began, slowly, to climb.
One the sun, two a slough, three TV, four no more, five
the sky, six a lie –Seven. Eight. Nine. Nine. It was a circle.
Where had it started? (*pause*) And then I heard it again,
that *sound*. A roar. Like a train, only louder. A sound rising
up from the mud-coloured river, like an ancient sleeping
sturgeon waking, and breaking open the sky. (*pause*) With
every rung of the ladder, it grew stronger. Twenty rungs,
twenty beads, spinning backwards and forwards, until I
stopped, turned around. (*pause*) Below me the workers
were coming off graveyard, trudging home in the morning
light, sawdust spilling from pant cuffs and collars, faces
dusty with the sweat of labour. And on the other side
of the dike, the river, and beside it the reserve, cut off

from the town like a severed limb. (*pause*) And holding
real tight to those green cedar railings, I crouched down,
leaned over, and ... and I let it go, let it go and watched
it fall, watching it trail and spin, like a circle of beads in
a woman's necklace, like fear, like spit ... like a chain of
smoke rings, disappearing, into the wet-grey smoky air.

Frog sounds, from under the seats of the
audience, slowly increase in volume.

TALKER
And a voice like the sound of many voices, rising up, rising
up in the mill-whistle morning. Up from the sawdust and
boxcars shunting, and the boys in the empty streets still
shouting, borne up, borne up from the howling dead, and
pulsing through my veins like a song:

"Hey Boys!
What do you say, eh boys?
Eh boys?
Eh boys?
Eh?"

THE END

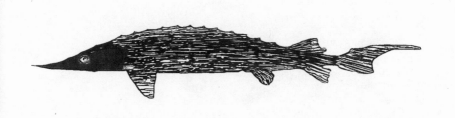

The Girl Who Swam Forever

by

MARIE CLEMENTS

PRODUCTION HISTORY

The Girl Who Swam Forever was first produced by Savage Media and the University of British Columbia in Vancouver, British Columbia, in 1995, with the following cast and crew:

FOREVER / THE GIRL   Cheri Maracle

RAY / BROTHER BIG EYES   Archer Pechawis

JIM / THE FISHERMAN   Fraser Mackenzie

GRANDMOTHER / THE OLD ONE   Agnes Pierre

THE CHURCH FROGS   Wayne Lavallee
                                         Jerry Longboat
                                         Rebecca Lee
                                         Fraser Mackenzie
                                         Stefany Mathias

Director   Nelson Gray
Set Designer   James Bailey
Lighting Designer   Susann Hudson
Costume Designer   Danica West
Composer   Greg Ray
Choreographers   Cathy Burnett and Nelson Gray
Composer of "Sturgeon Song"   Wayne Lavallee
Katzie Creation Story   Old Pierre of the Katzie People
                                 (retold by Agnes Pierre)

CHARACTERS

GRANDMOTHER / THE OLD ONE: The Girl's dead grandmother / An ancient Sturgeon. Old, gentle, and deep.

FOREVER / THE GIRL: A young Katzie girl of sixteen who is running from a Catholic mission school / The Girl-Sturgeon in myth. She has a dreamlike quality and moves with the ease of a fish.

RAY/BROTHER BIG EYES: The Girl's brother. Older and cooler. A great dancer / The Owl in the myth. Bird-like in movement and attitude.

JIM / THE FISHERMAN: The Girl's lover / A young non-Indigenous fisherman.

THE CHURCH FROGS: Voices of the church. Nightmarish. The church conscience of the Girl. They take bodies as nuns and priests, dressed in black with large frog heads.

SETTING

The play takes place both underwater and on land. Real and myth. Movement based. Using slides/video and soundscape to create both worlds.

TIME

Early sixties / The beginning.

The Katzie descended from the first people God created on Pitt Lake. The ruler was known as Clothed with Power. This first Chief had a son and a daughter. The daughter spent her days swimming and transformed into a sturgeon. The first fish to inhabit the Pitt Lake. It was from this girl that all sturgeons descended. After she left, her brother wept uncontrollably and Clothed with Power took the silk-like hair of the goat and transformed him into an owl-like bird that could only be seen by the Katzie descendants. It is only by human hand that a sturgeon can die and those that wish to take a sturgeon must first seek spirit power from her brother the white bird. Sometimes the sturgeon will make itself available to the fisherman. Sometimes a song must be chanted to which steam will emerge and the sturgeon will make themselves caught floating to the surface belly up.

—OLD PIERRE

It is said that the white sturgeon are somehow involved in the whereabouts of souls of those who drown and whose bodies are never recovered from the river.

—ROBERT JOE as quoted in
Terry Glavin's *A Ghost in the Water*

From the darkness a voice speaks – large, dark,
and old. A light splashes down into the darkness
creating a filter that shows layers of blue from the
highest/lightest to the darkest bottom. The light
rests on the face of THE OLD ONE. She rocks
in a rocking chair on the bottom of the river, the
light catching her face as she rocks to and fro.

THE OLD ONE
Sometimes you don't know your own story from the
bottom up or from the top down until it meets you.
Meets in you. Words and silence, swimming and falling to
the middle, circling each other in a dance of remembering.
A remembering transforming. A dream from the here and
now to the beginning, and again from the here and now to
the beginning again.

The light dims on THE OLD ONE. The
stage is left in darkness. Pairs of sturgeon
eyes appear from the darkness.

THE OLD ONE remains in the dark as the
GRANDMOTHER. A dim light is brought
up on a bed surface. It looks like mud but
is the figure of THE GIRL covered by a
blanket. A brief projected image of a sturgeon
on the blanket. It moves as the girl stirs.

THE OLD ONE
A story begins from the darkest part of us to the deepest.
From our unknown the lightest thing can surface. From

the youngest the oldest thing can be born. To know this thing is to name an instinct you had before you knew how it sounded. An instinct you had before you knew how you looked. You swam, you flew, you sang, you loved things that did not know you existed and some that did. This thing will come to you and ask to be heard, to be seen, to be loved, and that will make you bigger.

As FOREVER sits up, the sturgeon image
vanishes. Small bulges appear under the blankets.

FOREVER

It is hard to hide anything here. The smallest bulge can lead to a full day of prayers. The smallest apple stolen from the kitchen, the smallest piece of bread tucked inside, or under, can give you away. I can't sleep for trying to think about what I am going to do. I lie awake at night, night after night, and stare up into the ceiling and ask the darkness for an answer, but all I get is God's eyes looking at me, and it is not an answer he is giving me but a dirty look.

As she mouths words to a song, her
GRANDMOTHER sings the song softly,
finally reaching her hand over and gently
stroking her grandchild FOREVER's hair.

FOREVER

So I close my eyes hoping he won't be able to see me and I try to sing or mouth words that my Grandmother used to say to me when everything went dark. Dark when my father disappeared, dark when my mother disappeared, dark until all that was left was the sound of my grandmother's soft words and her hands coming, appearing out of that darkness, stroking my head and hair and tears, until those old hands took my pain in their creases and smoked them.

GRANDMOTHER's hands disappear.

FOREVER
I know my father and mother didn't really disappear but
it feels that way when people die. One minute they are
here, right here, and the next they are gone, just gone, and
no matter how far or hard you look for them they are
just gone. My father was swept away by the river and my
Grandmother says my mother ...

GRANDMOTHER
... couldn't take it anymore.

FOREVER
I wonder if she died of "I couldn't take it anymore."

*Light up on the hands of her GRANDMOTHER
intertwined, lying on her lap rocking in and
out of the light as she goes back and forth.*

FOREVER
My grandmother's soft words would end then and
she would take those smoking hands and weave them
together and leave them in the middle of her lap for the
longest time, her eyes bent on them, rocking a pain back
and forth. (*reaching out and touching those hands*) "It's
alright Grandma, it's alright." I try to remember everyone
sometimes. I remember my Grandmother best because
she disappeared not long ago, and sometimes I don't
think she's disappeared at all. I remember her hands and
the sound of her words. I remember pieces of everyone –
my father's strong arms pulling up fishnets, my mother's
long black hair, and my brother. I need to see my brother
just to make sure he hasn't disappeared and either have
I. This place can make you feel like everything has

disappeared. Tomorrow I'll take my leave of absence and steal as many apples and pieces of bread I want from the kitchen. I'll bulge out everywhere and run. I know they'll come after me but I'll go to places I remember and they don't know and maybe they won't find me this time. Sister Alphonse says that God sees everything. And I won't argue that, but he sees what I know, and I know he knows because I can feel him giving me a dirty look. He knows, but he hasn't told anybody here, and that's a good sign.

Darkness. The sound of a train approaching.
We hear it before we see it. A train light
blares on FOREVER like a confession light
getting brighter and brighter. The sound of the
train increases with growing intensity, wheels
turning and a train passing throughout.

FOREVER
Every time I see a train I feel like trying to catch it. I feel like running with it as fast as I can. Trying to keep up with it until the very moment it rushes past whispering that you could be part of it ... if you could just run fast enough.

THE OLD ONE
(*whispering as the train*) Run faster.

FOREVER
It whispers right in your ear and then swims past like it wanted to tell you something else but changed its mind. It leaves you like a giant sigh.

THE OLD ONE
(*whispering as the train*) We could have gone somewhere.

FOREVER

Anywhere. I think of my brother, words unspoken. I think
of Old Al's leg that was cut off by a train. I think I like my
body parts.

The sound and image of the train passing.

FOREVER

I watch it pass. I think about an Elder who wanted his
spirit guardian to be a locomotive because it was so strong
and made of steel. It had an iron history but could see the
future. I should have been made of steel.

*Sound of a train blast. The image of trees taking
over. FOREVER walks through the trees and sits
on a swing. FOREVER's eyes are closed, listening to
the woods and approaching steps. Voice-over replies
of "I don't know, I haven't seen her," etc., from the
reservation are heard under the action. The outline
of a boy hiding behind a tree and looking at her.*

FOREVER

I was swinging on the swing, swinging good-sounding lies
back and forth, trying to think – what to tell my brother,
when I felt those eyes on me. I kept my eyes closed so
I could hear the sound of leaves crying out crunch by
crunch ... getting closer ... smashing the upturned leaves
like hands curling and caught under a weight, foot by
noisy foot. (*to herself*) I hear you ... Do you think I have
no ears? (*yelling at him*) Hey, do you think I have no ears?
Quiet. Just the sound of his eyes on my body. You know,
blue eyes ... Eyes lookin' at you like you were some kind
of strange sight ... Like white boy eyes lookin' straight
at your private parts as you walk by. Quiet. It made me
madder and madder that he could look at me that way

and I was the one who was supposed to be embarrassed.
(*jumping from the swing and yelling in his direction again*)
*I'm gonna tell my brother you know. I'm gonna tell my brother
about you and if he doesn't get you, I will* ... Quiet.

> *Sound of leaf steps going and the
> increasing sound of frog ribbitting.*

FOREVER
Then the sound of fast-crunching leaves and frogs.
Someone saw me and they will talk ... talk up a damn
ribbit storm gossiping ... getting me caught. Damn him
and these damn noisy frogs. I could eat you little frogs.
I could stick you with a big pointy stick clear through and
barbecue you, so watch what you say.

> *The frogs become silent.*

FOREVER
Quiet. So quiet. Quiet. I felt guilty. I shouldn't have yelled.
So quiet I could hear my conscience getting closer and I
knew God had finally told them and they were looking for
me and they were getting closer.

> *The sound of the croaking frogs becomes more
> human-like – the voices of her church conscience.
> The outlines of priests and nuns appear between
> the trees. Their faces are revealed as frog faces. The
> sound and actions of THE CHURCH FROGS
> become nightmarish and menacing. A drum
> has been placed at the middle of FOREVER
> and the circle is being stretched painfully. The
> green of the forest fades into the dark red of roe
> taking centre on her stomach. They pull at her.*

FOREVER
Finally placing their hands on me. Tugging and pulling
and stretching a confession any way they could. Tugging
at my words and pulling them till I don't know what I just
said. Stretching any truth to lies. Pulling my body till this
bulbous middle shifts itself from fear. This fear moves in
me and dislodges this foaming guilt that makes me sick
every morning, scared everyone will see this bulge. I don't
tell them the skin on my stomach is starting to stretch like
I was making a drum. I don't tell them. I don't confess
anything. I don't tell anybody. Anything. They would
sneak peeks at my drum. I cover my belly.

> *A CHURCH FROG hits her stomach with a*
> *drumstick. A loud drumbeat sounds. FOREVER*
> *crouches doubled up and sick. The sound of leaves*
> *crunching and approaching steps. FOREVER*
> *hears them but doesn't look up. BROTHER*
> *BIG EYES walks to her. Throughout the scene*
> *FOREVER and BROTHER BIG EYES are*
> *moving from the forest to an abandoned boat.*

FOREVER
Ray?

BROTHER BIG EYES
Yeah. It's me. Are you okay?

FOREVER
Yeah.

BROTHER BIG EYES
You don't look okay.

FOREVER
I'm alright now. I just felt kinda sick, that's all.

BROTHER BIG EYES
You sure? How did you know it was me?

FOREVER
I didn't. How did you know it was me?

BROTHER BIG EYES
I didn't. I was just going to see if you were at the boat
and I heard all this frog racket and thought somebody
must be here. So I thought it might be you.

FOREVER
Oh.

BROTHER BIG EYES
So?

FOREVER
So what?

BROTHER BIG EYES
You know, so what? I wasn't expecting you 'til the holidays.

FOREVER
Why, you would have dressed for it?

BROTHER BIG EYES
At least shaved.

FOREVER
You're shaving now?

BROTHER BIG EYES
I was always shaving.

FOREVER
Now you were always shaving.

BROTHER BIG EYES
Okay, okay, I finally got this amazing growth.

FOREVER
Scary.

BROTHER BIG EYES
Besides being here, what's wrong?

FOREVER
Nothing. I just needed to see you. You know. I just needed
to ... I miss her. I thought maybe by being here ...

BROTHER BIG EYES
Yeah, I miss her too.

FOREVER
You should miss the way she dressed you.

BROTHER BIG EYES
She never dressed me ... Okay, she helped ... I like the way
I'm dressed.

FOREVER
Real Tough.

BROTHER BIG EYES
What?

FOREVER
I said you look real good. Really.

BROTHER BIG EYES
Well, you're not going to look too good with a bald head.

FOREVER
Only if they catch me. They said they were going to shave my head if I ran away again and they caught me. They are not going to catch me this time.

BROTHER BIG EYES
You better hope not because you'd look really ugly with no hair.

FOREVER
I think I'd still look pretty good.

BROTHER BIG EYES
O yeah, they'll be lining up to marry you. Your only hope would be to marry Old Al.

FOREVER
Perfect. He has no teeth and he has a wooden leg.

BROTHER BIG EYES
Well, you are getting older and if they catch you you'll have no hair. I think you'd make a real pretty bald, legless couple and have real ugly babies.

FOREVER
Thanks.

She turns away.

BROTHER BIG EYES
What's wrong?

FOREVER
Nothing.

BROTHER BIG EYES
I was just kidding.

FOREVER
I know.

BROTHER BIG EYES
Hey ... Don't worry ... We'll think of something. Maybe
they're tired of running after you.

FOREVER
Ray?

BROTHER BIG EYES
Do you ever see Grandma?

BROTHER BIG EYES
Forever?

FOREVER
Don't look at me that way. I know she's dead but do you
ever see her?

BROTHER BIG EYES
No but sometimes I can feel her and sometimes I think
I dream of her when I'm sleeping but when I wake
up I can't remember the dream but I feel like she was
there. Just for a second. You're not gonna go all weird on
me are you?

FOREVER
Too late.

BROTHER BIG EYES
Way too late ... Well, I should go see how the search
party is doing. They'll be looking for me to say my
good words ... "No I don't know where she is. Do you
think I'm lying?"

FOREVER
When are you coming back?

BROTHER BIG EYES
As soon as I can. You'll be alright here.

FOREVER
Yeah, I know.

BROTHER BIG EYES
I'll bring you some stuff. You okay? You sure?

FOREVER
Yeah, sure.

> FOREVER sits under the abandoned hull of a
> boat that is made of the ribs of a fish skeleton.
> BROTHER BIG EYES goes to leave and then
> stops and watches her settle into the hull of the
> boat without knowing that he is watching her.

BROTHER BIG EYES
I could feel she wasn't telling me everything. I could feel a
change. I thought maybe they had done some things with
her at the mission school that she didn't think she could
tell me. Some things that nobody here wanted to hear but

it came out anyway. Came out in strange ways. In mothers crying through the night and fathers loading and reloading their guns and then simply having to put them down, placing them down, the weight of having to put them down, the weight of that moment of helplessness leaving a hunch in their backs forever. The weight of that rage never leaving their bodies. It wasn't their way. It wasn't our way. Would it be my way? I don't know. Rage comes easy to me. It bunches up in my fists heavy until I let them fly. In this flying I come to understand a power. I know it is a power misused but I feel this power and it feels old, and I know it knows me, and knows what I am up against, and comes to me to make the fight an honest one, or at least even. At least even.

BROTHER BIG EYES exits.

FOREVER gets comfortable in the boat.
A blue light fades up on the hull of the boat.
FOREVER dips her foot in and then her body
and finally is submerged in the colour of water.

FOREVER

Now that I'm here, I can't stop thinking about him. Thinking about the first time I saw him. I'd seen him before, everybody here has seen everybody before. But it was the first time I really saw him. And I think it was the first time anybody had really seen me.

A light dims up on the water tower and reveals
the shadowy figure of a man looking down.

FOREVER

I was just getting out of the water after a swim. And I felt something looking at me.

FOREVER looks up at him. JIM climbs
down and crosses the track to the other side.

FOREVER
Somebody looking at me. Somebody was way up on
the water tower looking down. We looked at each other.
I couldn't see his face but a body that positioned itself so
comfortable, so arrogantly there like he thought he was an
eagle or something and at any moment he could leave ...
He came down from the tower and walked over to me
and just said "Hi."

JIM
Hi.

FOREVER
Just like that. He said he'd been watching me swim.
He said he'd been watching me swim every day for a few
days and that I looked like I could really swim.

JIM
You look like you were born to swim.

FOREVER
I said, "What were you born to do?" He said he was ...

JIM
... "Born to be wild."

FOREVER
We laughed. But it was more than that. It's that feeling you
get when you meet someone and know that you are different
from each other because it's obvious, but what makes you
stand and stare is that you know you are the same in ways
that you can't explain yet – you just recognize each other.

Scene fades with FOREVER and JIM just
standing and looking at each other.

BROTHER BIG EYES stands on the railroad
tracks with his foot on either side of the town.
He carries a bag full of food to give to FOREVER.

BROTHER BIG EYES
I can feel them talking. I can't always make out what
they're saying but I can tell they're talking and talking,
and that talking has something to do with something they
don't know anything about. Sometimes that talking comes
with a laughter. A laughter that comes out and then turns
its head on you, and turns into a whisper. That whisper
turns into a hush. Some kind of civilized hush ... that I
wish I could break. I feel they're talking not about me but
about mine but I can't hear it all, and it makes me nervous.
Edgy. It makes me think this has something to do with
Forever and that ... that is ... not acceptable. My sister is
not for them to even talk about. Somebody's been where
they shouldn't be. Because I can feel them talking about it.
They know something I don't know and that is dangerous.

FOREVER sits in the hull of the boat
looking out over the water. BROTHER
BIG EYES watches her and walks in.

BROTHER BIG EYES
Hey, how come you look so sad? What's wrong?

FOREVER
Nothing.

BROTHER BIG EYES
Oh come on – it's me.

FOREVER
  It's not important.

BROTHER BIG EYES
  Forever?

FOREVER
  What?

BROTHER BIG EYES
  Why did you run away this time?

        No response.

  Forever!

        *BROTHER BIG EYES goes to push
        her playfully and winds up a punch.*

FOREVER
  Like hell, try it. (*winding up*)

BROTHER BIG EYES
  Don't swear.

FOREVER
  Don't tell me how to talk.

BROTHER BIG EYES
  Didn't those priests and nuns teach you nothin'?

FOREVER
  Nothing. Didn't they teach you nothing?

BROTHER BIG EYES
Nothing for years and look at me now.

FOREVER
Yeah ... Look at you now.

BROTHER BIG EYES
They're still out there looking for you, you know.

FOREVER
I know.

BROTHER BIG EYES
And sooner or later they'll find you.

FOREVER
I don't think so.

BROTHER BIG EYES
And take you back to ...

FOREVER
Straight back to ...

BROTHER BIG EYES
To ...

FOREVER
Divinity.

BROTHER BIG EYES
Scary word!

FOREVER
It's a scary place ...

    Beat.

BROTHER BIG EYES
Did something happen there?

FOREVER
Just the usual.

BROTHER BIG EYES
I don't know then ... Is this about a guy, Forever? If it is
I'll tell them where you are myself.

FOREVER
No you wouldn't.

BROTHER BIG EYES
Don't push me.

FOREVER
OOOOooo now that's scary. What makes you think
it's a guy?

BROTHER BIG EYES
What makes you think I'm so stupid?

FOREVER
I won't answer that.

BROTHER BIG EYES
If it wasn't a guy you'd have already told me
what was wrong.

FOREVER
Maybe it's none of your business.

BROTHER BIG EYES
You're my business.

FOREVER
Why?

BROTHER BIG EYES
Because I'm your brother.

FOREVER
So?

BROTHER BIG EYES
So tell me about it?

FOREVER
I can't ... yet ... Things are just changing that's all.
I'm changing.

BROTHER BIG EYES
Changing ... What does changing mean?

FOREVER
I never used to have to explain things to you.

BROTHER BIG EYES
I never used to have to ask. Do I know him? It's a him
isn't it? This whole thing is about a him isn't it?

FOREVER
No it isn't.

BROTHER BIG EYES
Don't lie.

FOREVER
I'm not lying.

BROTHER BIG EYES
Well, I hope he knows who your brother is. Because if you ran away to be with some asshole you're both going to be sorry. Do you hear me, Forever?

FOREVER
No ... Of course I hear you, you're yelling right at me.

BROTHER BIG EYES.
I'm not yelling.

FOREVER
Yes you are.

BROTHER BIG EYES
No I'm not.

FOREVER
Yes you are ... Ray, I missed you too.

BROTHER BIG EYES
I didn't say I missed you.

FOREVER
You didn't have to.

BROTHER BIG EYES
Yeah, well, I'll see you later. I got some things to take care of.

FOREVER
Like what?

BROTHER BIG EYES
It's none of your business.

> *BROTHER BIG EYES exits. FOREVER*
> *lays down in the boat and falls asleep.*

> *Dream Music Filters Up. The boat begins*
> *to rock with the music. Just the hands of*
> *her GRANDMOTHER steering the motion.*
> *Water light dims and fills the stage to a deepwater*
> *darkness filtering light. FOREVER floats down*
> *into the dream – the river. THE OLD ONE*
> *takes her place at the bottom of the riverbed in*
> *her rocking chair. A sturgeon image grows from*
> *her, making her bigger and bigger as she talks.*

THE OLD ONE
A hundred years I have been talking but no one has
listened. I weigh eight hundred pounds with words
spoken but not heard. Eight hundred pounds I have
grown one hundred years to reach you but still nothing.
Nothing until I heard my voice swimming inside you.
I took those eight hundred pounds of silence and spun
them in years of circles to create you. You are made of
words in my silence. You are made of a silence that is me
before everything.

FOREVER
I do not see well here.

> *BROTHER BIG EYES floats by on a bicycle.*

FOREVER
It is dark like a great dream.

THE CHURCH FROGS *count apples.*

FOREVER
I cast my shadow and the bottom of my world
moves fishlike.

FOREVER moves. Her shadow is larger
than her girl-body, and sturgeon-like. Similar
sturgeon shadows gather around her.

FOREVER
That is all I have to understand.

Garbage descends down to the river
bottom. Beer bottles, an old boot, a bicycle
wheel, bones, flecks of sawdust.

THE OLD ONE
It is crowded here with all that has been discarded. There
are my people, some bone white from the journey. Some
calling to join us from under the sawdust. Some – still
some – large with words unspoken. It is crowded here
with all that has been discarded ... sunken boats and
bones and me ... sunken boats and bones and me.

FOREVER
It is cold here. And hot here. And cold when it should be
hot, and hot when it should be cold.

THE OLD ONE
No one knows where to dream anymore. No one knows
where a million-year-old dream can go. So we rise up

to lay on your banks, not because we have given up but because we are dreaming of a new beginning.

> *FOREVER rises up with the light and returns to her sleeping form.*

FOREVER
(*in sleep*) Grandma?

> *Blackout. BROTHER BIG EYES enters from a high perch and looks down on FOREVER as she sleeps. He takes the drum and stirs a thinking circle. He slowly lays the drum down and falls asleep on his perch.*
>
> *JIM approaches FOREVER and wakes her gently. The following scene is more about what isn't said than what is.*

FOREVER
Hey ...

JIM
Hi ... What are you doing here?

FOREVER
What are you doing here? You first.

JIM
I heard you might be, or somebody might be down here somewhere.

FOREVER
Who did you hear it from? My brother?

JIM
If I heard it from your brother I don't think I'd be here.

FOREVER
Right. I wanted to … talk … talk to you …

JIM
I was thinking about you.

FOREVER
I need to tell you something and it's real …

JIM
About …

FOREVER
Us … Oh God/… (Shit did I say)

JIM
/Oh shit.

FOREVER
/God.

JIM
You wanted to talk to me about God.

FOREVER
You wanted to talk to me about Shit.

FOREVER
No/…

JIM
/No … I just wanted to know you were okay.

FOREVER
Are you okay?

JIM
I think so. (*long pause*)

> *JIM slowly, silently digs in his pocket and*
> *puts his rosary beads in her hands.*

FOREVER
He knew but he didn't want to know. He didn't want to
hear the words. I started crying. I couldn't help myself.
He put his rosary beads into my hands ...

> *A drumbeat comes in softly and then louder as a*
> *heartbeat, mixed with water sounds, a low song.*

FOREVER
Do you think these will help? ... Small round cool beads
in my sweating hands ... Do *you* think these will help? ...
That's when *his* hands started sweating. He just stared at
me. Quiet for a long time. So quiet he was almost begging
me not to tell him so I just sat there and he just sat down.
Me wishing he would say something and him wishing I
wouldn't say anything. So quiet I started listening to my
insides. I could hear Grandmother's voice inside me. Right
inside my stomach with it. Listening, guggling, bubbling
through my veins. Not so much words but a song she
used to sing to me when I was a kid and scared. Vibrating
through my body like the heartbeat of a drum. He got
quieter. I asked him if he could hear anything.

FOREVER
Can you hear anything?

JIM
No.

FOREVER
No? No ... I wasn't about to tell him about my
Grandmother there inside me too ... he looked scared
enough. I wanted to tell him, to ask him ... to say ...

JIM
I can't hear a thing.

FOREVER
You can't hear a thing. I know. I know ...

FOREVER and JIM stare at each other.

He looked at me like he felt sorry for me. I looked at
him the same.

*JIM finally exits. FOREVER lies back
down and holds herself. She falls asleep.*

Dream Music: Old to New.

*THE OLD ONE enters speaking in Katzie and
English. She takes her place as the storyteller in her
rocking chair. BROTHER BIG EYES wakes up
in his dream. He places the drum in the sky and
raises it to become a moon. BROTHER BIG EYES
dives into the water as FOREVER falls into it.*

*FOREVER and BROTHER BIG EYES
echo some of the Katzie words, remembering
fragments of their language.*

FOREVER
I am dreaming.

BROTHER BIG EYES
I am dreaming.

THE OLD ONE
The Lord Above gave my forefather a wife by whom he
had two offspring, a son and daughter. These children
never ate food, but spent all their days in the water –

> *FOREVER and BROTHER BIG EYES begin
> to move in slow motion, as if through water.*

FOREVER and BROTHER BIG EYES
I remember the river.

THE OLD ONE
"My friends," he said, "you know that my daughter spends
all her days in the water. For the benefit of generations to
come, I have decided she shall remain there forever."

BROTHER BIG EYES
Forever?

THE OLD ONE
He led her to the water's edge and said, "My daughter, you
are enamoured of the water. For the benefit of generations
to come, I shall now change you into a sturgeon."

> *FOREVER begins to transform and
> move like a sturgeon; the image of a
> sturgeon appears on her as she moves.*

THE GIRL
I am floating under the water softly.

THE OLD ONE
"Thus the Sturgeon was created in Pitt Lake, the first fish that ever ruffled its waters."

THE GIRL
I do not see well here. It is dark.

THE OLD ONE
"Oetectaan's son mourned so inconsolably for his sister that at last the father summoned the people again."

> *BROTHER BIG EYES transforms into an owl.*
> *He takes his place on his perch as an owl. He grabs*
> *the moon and begins drumming with the music.*

THE OLD ONE
"He plucked the finest and silkiest hair from the mountain goat, laid it on the boy's head and limbs and transformed him into a bird. 'Fly away,' he said. 'Hereafter the man who wishes to capture your sister, the Sturgeon, shall seek power from you.'"

THE GIRL and BROTHER BIG EYES
It is far down, this dream.

BROTHER BIG EYES
I see everything.

THE GIRL
I cast my shadow and the bottom of my world moves fishlike.

BROTHER BIG EYES
I cast my shadow and the bottom of my world moves under my wings.

THE OLD ONE
Sometimes the sturgeon will make itself available to a fisherman.

> *"Last Kiss" fades up and over original Dream Music. BROTHER BIG EYES, seeing THE FISHERMAN and hearing the strange music tries to drum as loud as the song. Lights fade him out musically and visually.*

> *Lights up on JIM as a fisherman on the water tower. THE FISHERMAN lowers his fishing line – a long huge string of rosary beads – and lifts FOREVER up. Sturgeon images dance on the screen around them.*

FOREVER
I like to dance and you like to pray and sometimes when you fall you fall for me and we dance. Oh we dance.

> *FOREVER and JIM embrace and discover each other. He lifts her up and a cloud of steam covers them.*

THE OLD ONE
Sometimes a song must be chanted to which steam will emerge and the sturgeon will make herself caught floating to the surface belly up.

> *Underwater sex scene.*

FOREVER
I am so close to hearing your words.
I am too close.
I am so close to believing your words.
I am suffocating.
I am so close to your words I can't hear that
your words have become a hook.
I swallow those words.
Some bubbling from your mouth.
Some coming from your eyes.
I swallow them all.
Blue-sky eyes and all.
Swallow 'til they reach the bottom of me where
everything is silent and still. Unspeakable
and dark. I have fallen for your words and you
have fallen into me.

> Steam finally takes over the stage
> and covers everything but the image
> of THE OLD ONE rocking.

THE OLD ONE
It is said that the white sturgeon are somehow involved in
the souls of those who drown and whose bodies are never
recovered from the river.

> THE OLD ONE disappears. Whiteness fades
> and leaves FOREVER waking up trying to
> surface from the dream, confused by her form.

FOREVER
I came up between the log booms, sticks squishing each side
of me till I became smaller and browner, and they became as
wide as a forest, few breaths in between. I had been dreaming
to the top and got caught between the worlds.

*BROTHER BIG EYES drops from
his perch and confronts her.*

BROTHER BIG EYES
Forever?

FOREVER
What?

BROTHER BIG EYES
It is him isn't it?

FOREVER
Him who?

BROTHER BIG EYES
Jim Harding.

FOREVER
Jim who?

BROTHER BIG EYES
You slept with him didn't you?

FOREVER
You don't understand.

BROTHER BIG EYES
What's to understand?

FOREVER
If you just let me explain/

BROTHER BIG EYES
/Explain what, that my sister is sleeping with every
guy in town?

FOREVER
It's not like that.

BROTHER BIG EYES
No let me guess ... you're in love ... you are both in love
and you're gonna get married. You're sixteen. He's white
for Christ's sake.

FOREVER
It's not about that.

BROTHER BIG EYES
What's it about? Do you want to tell me what it is about?
What! Let me guess, this white guy is going to take you
away from all of this, is that right, is that right, is that what
he said, "Huh"?

FOREVER
He didn't say anything.

BROTHER BIG EYES
I could feel them talking you know ... talking all over
my back as if I couldn't see who left their looks on me.
Talking all the time and all the time it's you this is about
you and some guy you let touch you. Everybody knows,
Forever. EVERYBODY and the whole town will know by
now. Look at you. Look at what he's done to you. Gave
you a little more than you expected didn't he?

FOREVER
Stop it.

FOREVER tries to cover herself.

BROTHER BIG EYES
Didn't he?

FOREVER
What ... Don't look at me what way.

BROTHER BIG EYES
You're pregnant aren't you?

No response.

BROTHER BIG EYES
Aren't you? Tell me the truth!

FOREVER
I always tell the truth. Yes ... Yes! Alright.

BROTHER BIG EYES
Did you tell him? What did he say?

FOREVER
/I think he knows but ...

BROTHER BIG EYES
What did the great man say?

FOREVER
He didn't say anything.

BROTHER BIG EYES
I'll change that. He'll have a lot to say ...

FOREVER
Ray, don't –

BROTHER BIG EYES
Ray don't what???

FOREVER
Don't ... Don't do this ... Calm down ...

She tries to settle him down.

BROTHER BIG EYES
It's already done ... Don't touch me. Don't come near me.

FOREVER
You promised you'd always be there ... You promised
you'd never disappear. Please Ray, you're the only one
left I ... can ...

BROTHER BIG EYES stops and
is about to give in but leaves.

FOREVER wanders through space, lost
and trying to put herself together.

FOREVER
(whispering) I can ... I can ... I can ...

The area turns green. Sound of rain coming down
and THE CHURCH FROGS. FOREVER is wet
and standing in the forest. THE CHURCH FROGS
croak soft prayers of baptism, then louder and harsher
prayer. They should be under the following but rise
to it and her desperation. An image of FOREVER as
the mission schoolgirl appears on her or the chorus.

THE CHURCH FROGS
You kneel down on the floor in front of everybody. Tell
them you're sorry you ran away. You're no different than
the rest of them! How we gonna beat the devil out of
you ... The devil is strong in you. So strong. Are you
feeling dirty because of what happened? These wild little
Indian pagans.

FOREVER
I was baptizing myself in the rain asking forgiveness for
the fact. I thought the rain would stream down my body
in rivers and make me clean again. Stream down my
hair, my eyes, my neck, downstream over my breasts to
the middle of me. The very middle. My own ceremony.
Drops of holy water washing. No priest for me this time.
No confession. Just me and the Virgin Mary talking
straight 'cause I thought she might understand because
she had a baby even though she was a virgin. Anyways,
it doesn't hurt to ask.

> *The image of FOREVER as a woman*
> *appears. The woman is sexual and nude.*
> *FOREVER lays the beads over herself.*

FOREVER
I took my lover's beads so I could wear them day in and
day out. I wore them so I could feel them lay on top of
me. The cross at the end stretching and pointing below
my belly reminding me. My first time with a man. I wore
them so I could count each bead according to what I was
praying for. Him or me. Or him with me. Or me with
memory of him between my legs ...

> *Image of FOREVER large with pregnancy.*

FOREVER
I wonder if I could unhook this child from me, this dream from me. If I could pull the pieces from me that did not fit. Red fleshy bits of blood and me left at the end of a hook and weighing down on this webbed net ... I could've gutted myself right there just to see if like a fish I would die swift and spineless, mercifully headless. No dream, just the red stain of blood left on the pier joining the other stains of death ingrained into the wood. (*taking the beads, about to stab herself with a cross*) If I could take this knife and cut the ancient and new from me. Cut the circle from my gut and take that circle, wash it in the river and see what it is made of. Is it flesh, my flesh? Or dreams that do not fit between these worlds.

The image of a sturgeon appears on her.

When it is all said and done throw my bones in the river, brother ... This place is too hungry and greedy and needy for me. Throw my bones in the river. I have given all I know ... and leave knowing nothing. Throw my bones in the river, throw my bones in the river brother ... Hurry I want to go home!

The shadow of THE OLD ONE / STURGEON comes from behind her, fishlike. THE CHURCH FROGS back away and fade. GRANDMOTHER's hand reaches in the light and gently rests on FOREVER's head and strokes her hair. She sings softly.

GRANDMOTHER
It will be alright ... shhh ... It will be alright. I am here Forever. I am here ... (*placing her hand on FOREVER's stomach*) Here. Here. These pieces, these stories have

found a place in you. Found a place to grow from the beginning and circle to include everything that is you and circle to include everything that is us. Here. Here. It circles and in this motion a million year old dream surfaces. A dream that is being made smaller by the loudness of a dream silenced. Here. Here. Let this dream breathe. Let its breath flow in you, taking you, shaping you with its memory and your future. Here. Here you will grow stronger. Here. Here you will grow larger in the knowledge it will never disappear from you. Here. Here. Let us swim. Here. Here. Let us dream. Let us dream. Let us swim away on land.

> *The sound of a train approaching in the distance getting closer. The train's mechanical sound is mixed with the low sound of the sturgeon. FOREVER turns and runs for it.*
>
> *BROTHER BIG EYES is searching frantically for FOREVER.*

FOREVER
All I know was that I was running.

THE OLD ONE
All I know was that she was swimming.

BROTHER BIG EYES
Forever!

FOREVER
Running and then swimming forward.

BROTHER BIG EYES
Come back ... Come back. I didn't mean it.

FOREVER
  Running and running ...

THE OLD ONE
  Swimming and swimming ...

BROTHER BIG EYES
  Seeing everything but her.

FOREVER
  Falling into place.

BROTHER BIG EYES
  Forever!

THE OLD ONE
  She fell from the sky and landed here large.

FOREVER
  Swimming.

THE OLD ONE
  Bigger than your mind can imagine.

FOREVER
  Reaching out and away.

THE OLD ONE
  Longer than her black braids.

BROTHER BIG EYES
  Where are you?

THE OLD ONE
  Quieter than your conscience.

BROTHER BIG EYES
I'm here for you.

THE OLD ONE
More patient than a human century.

BROTHER BIG EYES
I'll be right here waiting for you.

FOREVER
Running and swimming.

BROTHER BIG EYES
Seeing you.

THE OLD ONE
Swimming and swimming.

FOREVER
Like steel.

> *We see FOREVER catching a train. Image*
> *of her looking out of a train. The train*
> *becomes a white sturgeon and a train,*
> *a white sturgeon and train, white sturgeon,*
> *train. Like it is dancing between the two.*

BROTHER BIG EYES
Pieces flying together.

THE OLD ONE
Stories meeting.

FOREVER
And swimming away on land.

BROTHER BIG EYES
  Getting smaller and smaller.

THE OLD ONE
  Circling in you.

FOREVER
  Taking everything.

THE OLD ONE
  Into a beginning.

BROTHER BIG EYES
  Disappearing.

FOREVER
  Into the city.

> *The sturgeon train gets smaller and disappears
> from sight. BROTHER BIG EYES takes the moon
> from the sky and drums and sings. Water sounds
> fade up. Owl-like he perches. His song becomes a
> wailing and begins to mix with tears of the rain.*

BROTHER BIG EYES
  I'll wait for you. I'll be right here waiting for you.

THE OLD ONE
  She was a watery thought one murky night. She formed
  out of our insistence. Taking shape and shore. Taking
  pleasure, conceiving a dream for the Old Ones. A dream
  that has washed up alive on our banks. Changing form but
  not intention. We dream a new beginning to this end.

> *Image of a train entering the city.*

FOREVER
(*voice-over*) I am swimming, Grandma. I am going to
have this baby, this dream. Maybe it will have blue eyes
and brown skin. Blue eyes so it won't have to stare at us
anymore because it would know us, because it would
know itself.

*The carcass of a sturgeon is strung up and cut
open. The image and the cry of a new child.
A leaping sturgeon. THE OLD ONE laughs.*

THE BEGINNING.

ACKNOWLEDGMENTS

TALKER'S TOWN

Many people contributed to the writing of *Talker's Town*. Thanks to Marie Clements, of course, and to the Katzie People. Greg Ray worked extensively as a researcher and script consultant, contributing enormously to the early writing stages. He worked with me to conduct a number of interviews with the Katzie People and with many other residents who had worked and grown up in and around Maple Ridge during the 1950s and early '60s. The results of these interviews – an oral history that we recorded and which is housed in the Maple Ridge Public Library – was a primary source in the writing of *Talker's Town*. I drew extensively on these interviews, quoting many passages verbatim, adapting others, and weaving them throughout the action and dialogue. My gratitude goes out to all of these people from Pitt Meadows, Hammond, and Maple Ridge for allowing their voices to inform this play. Thanks, as well, to Catriona Strang for her expert copy-editing in the final stages of the script.

THE GIRL WHO SWAM FOREVER

The playwright is indebted to Wayne Suttles and Diamond Jenness, editors of *Katzie Ethnographic Notes & Faith of a Coast Salish Indian*. The Genesis story, the second dream in *The Girl Who Swam Forever*, is taken from Old Pierre's retelling of the original story. Thanks also to Terry Glavin for *A Ghost in the Water*, published by New Star Books; to Agnes Pierre and the Pierre family; to Nelson Gray, author of *Talker's Town*. "*The Sturgeon Song*" was written and composed by Wayne Lavallee. Finally, thanks to the Westminster Fish Company.

NELSON GRAY is a playwright, theatre scholar, and professor in the English Department at Vancouver Island University. His interdisciplinary performances and collaborations with Lee Eisler have won numerous commissions and awards and have been produced in Canada, the United States, England, and Germany. He was the co-founder, with Beth Carruthers, of the Songbird Project – one of the first eco-art projects in Canada to bring together the arts, sciences, and community activists – and his poetry and scholarly articles have appeared in several journals and anthologies. With the assistance of a Canada Council Award and a SHHRC Insight Development Grant, he is currently working on the script and pre-production for *Here Oceans Roar*, a contemporary eco-opera based on his experiences as a salmon troller in the Pacific Northwest and on oceanographic research from Ocean Networks Canada.

MARIE CLEMENTS is an award-winning Métis performer, playwright, and director whose work has been presented on stages across Canada, the United States, and Europe. She is the founder of Urban Ink productions, a Vancouver-based First Nations production company that creates, develops and produces Aboriginal and multicultural works of theatre, dance, music, film, and video.